SHARK SCHOOL

3-Books-in-1! #2

READ ALL THE SHARK SCHOOL BOOKS!

SHARK SCHOOL

3-Books-in-1! #2

THE BOY WHO CRIED SHARK · A FIN-TASTIC FINISH · SPLASH DANCE

BY DAVY OCEAN
ILLUSTRATED BY AARON BLECHA

ALADDIN   New York   London   Toronto   Sydney   New Delhi

WiTH THANKS TO PAUL EBBS

ALADDIN

An imprint of Simon & Schuster Children's Publishing Division
1230 Avenue of the Americas, New York, New York 10020
This Aladdin paperback edition October 2018
The Boy Who Cried Shark text and concept copyright © 2013 by Hothouse Fiction
The Boy Who Cried Shark interior illustrations copyright © 2013 by Aaron Blecha
Originally published as *Harry Hammer: Shark Alert* in 2013 in Great Britain by Templar Publishing.
A Fin-tastic Finish text and concept copyright © 2014 by Hothouse Fiction
A Fin-tastic Finish interior illustrations copyright © 2014 by Aaron Blecha
Originally published as *Shark Camp* in 2014 in Great Britain by Templar Publishing.
Splash Dance text and concept copyright © 2014 by Hothouse Fiction
Splash Dance interior illustrations copyright © 2014 by Aaron Blecha
Originally published as *Shark Party* in 2014 in Great Britain by Templar Publishing.
Cover illustrations copyright © 2014 by Aaron Blecha
All rights reserved, including the right of reproduction in whole or in part in any form.
ALADDIN and related logo are registered trademarks of Simon & Schuster, Inc.
For information about special discounts for bulk purchases, please contact
Simon & Schuster Special Sales at 1-866-506-1949 or business@simonandschuster.com.
The Simon & Schuster Speakers Bureau can bring authors to your live event. For more
information or to book an event contact the Simon & Schuster Speakers Bureau at 1-866-248-3049
or visit our website at www.simonspeakers.com.
Series designed by Karin Paprocki
Interior designed by Mike Rosamilia
The text of this book was set in Write Demibd.
Manufactured in the United States of America 0918 OFF
2 4 6 8 10 9 7 5 3 1
Library of Congress Control Number 2018934203
ISBN 978-1-5344-3329-8 (pbk)
ISBN 978-1-4814-0690-1 (*The Boy Who Cried Shark* eBook)
ISBN 978-1-4814-0693-2 (*A Fin-tastic Finish* eBook)
ISBN 978-1-4814-0697-0 (*Splash Dance* eBook)
These titles were previously published individually.

Contents

The Boy Who Cried Shark

CHAPTER 1

Zoooooooooooooooooooooooooooooom!

Out of my room . . .

Screeeeeeeeeeeeeeeeeeeeeeech!

Down the stairs . . .

Ziiiiiiiiiiiiiiiiiiiiiiiiiiiiiiiiiiiiiiiiiiiiingg!

Into the hall . . .

YOOOOOOOOOOOOOOOOWLLLL!!!

"Sorry, Puddles!" I call back as I crash into our moth-eared catfish, sending him spinning out of control and bouncing into the wall. I don't stop to find out if he's all right. I must get to the jellyfishion before Mom and Dad!

It's Saturday night, and if I don't get there RIGHT NOW, they'll put on the news or some terrible sappy movie. They've been washing the dishes while I've been cleaning my room. There's always a rush to get to the den first after dinner, but tonight I *have* to get there first. So, instead of doing a total cleanup, I used my tail to sweep the mess under my bed. If Mom doesn't look too closely, I might just get away with it.

I come to the end of the hall, hook my dorsal on the doorframe, spin sideways (so my goofy hammery head doesn't get stuck in the door), and then—WHAM!—I'm in the den. Before Mom and Dad. YES!

Sailing around tail first, I slide into the finchair closest to the flat-screen jellyfishion and reach out with the flukes on my tail to flick the remote control off the coffee table and—

CLICK!

—down on the on button.

With a shiver and a fizz, the jellyfishion comes to life and I left-hammer the three button, just in time to see the judges for *The Shark Factor* being introduced. Pumping music blares and lasers burst across the stage, lighting the huge undersea set. The announcer, with his big, booming whale-size voice, waits for the pumping music to stop and then shouts out the names of the judges as they appear.

"Paddy!"

That's Paddy Snapper, the saltwater crocodile from Emerald Island. He slithers down the ramp on his yellow belly.

"Ellie!"

That's Ellie Electra, the smooth-bodied electric eel with ultra-shiny skin. She shimmies down the ramp and wraps herself around Paddy.

"Bobby!"

That's Bobby Barnacle, who is so tiny, he slides down the ramp under his own

personal magnifying glass so that everyone can see him.

"Marcus!"

And lastly, it's Marcus Sea-cow, wearing his trademark leather pants. He
waves his pink tail at the audience, and

with ocean-size smiles the four judges float to their huge clamshell seats.

"Oh no. Not this."

I look around at the sound of Dad's voice. He and Mom are swimming in from the kitchen. I grip the remote control tightly.

"I was hoping to catch some of my interview on the news," Dad says. Dad is mayor of Shark Point, and there's nothing he likes better than seeing himself on jellyfishion.

Mom flops down on to the sea-sponge sofa and groans. "Harry, do we have to watch this trash?"

Most weeks I wouldn't have minded. I mean, there are only so many times you can watch a fish being told he sings like a ship's horn that's got a seagull stuck in it. But this week . . . oh, man . . . this week I *have* to see the special guest who's opening the show.

10

We've been talking about it all week at school. Me, Ralph (my pilot-fish friend), and Joe (my jellyfish pal) have been finding it really difficult to concentrate in class. In the end, our teachers had to ban anyone from even mentioning *The Shark Factor*.

"But, Mom," I say, "I *have* to watch it tonight."

"Why?" she says, looking puzzled.

I let out a massive sigh. "Seriously, Mom, if you were any more uncool, we'd have to stick you on an iceberg. Gregor the Gnasher is singing his *first ever* single tonight."

My stomach is doing little flips just thinking about it. Gregor the Gnasher is a great white shark and my number-one hero. Not only is he the Underwater Wrestling Champion of the World (signature move: the fin-chop with tail-driver), he's also an action-movie star and now he's breaking into the music business as a rapper called G-White.

Tonight's performance has been the talk of the interwet, and the number of 'GREGOR' fan pages on Plaicebook has tripled in two days—making the system crash.

Marcus Sea-cow floats up from behind his desk.

"Ladies and gentlefish, welcome to *The Shark Factor!*"

The crowd goes wild.

Marcus Sea-cow grins and gestures to the stage. "And now, opening the show with his debut single, 'Bite It,' please welcome the one, the only, Geeeeeeeeeee-White!"

Horns ring out across the stage. Then comes the beat of drums. Search-lights start flashing through the water. A huge, glittery curtain opens at the back of the stage and there's Gregor, floating fin-high on a column of bubbles. Two dolphins wearing shiny dresses are dancing on either side of him. Around his neck is a big gold shark's tooth, hanging on a gold chain that's so thick, it looks as

if it came from the anchor of a cruise ship. He's wearing a red Shike track-suit with diamond-encrusted sneakers on each fluke of his tail.

Oh, man!

The audience has gone crazy. I sneak my tail toward the remote to turn the volume up. Sea-cow, Barnacle, Electra, and Snapper float up above their judges' desk and start clapping along.

G-White nods to the beat as the dol-phins sway beside him.

"I've got a big bite cuz I'm a great white," he raps.

I have to put my fin across my mouth to stop myself from squealing like a girl-shark.

"Great white!" the audience shouts back to him.

G-White grins, showing every single one of his three thousand and seventeen teeth. "I love causing FRIGHT, cuz I'm a great white!"

"Great white!" I join in with the audience.

"He's not too bright, he's a goofy great white," Dad mutters.

Huh?

I turn around and glare at Dad. He's shaking his head as he looks at the screen.

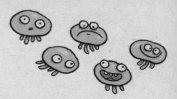

"Well, look at him," Dad says. "He might have lots of teeth, but I bet he couldn't think his way out of a wet paper bag."

"Dad!"

"Oh, come on, Harry. It's not exactly poetry, is it?" Dad says. "In my day we had real singers. Fish like Sting Ray and Sealion Dion. Now she could reach those high notes. This fool couldn't pitch a tent, let alone a tune."

Now Mom's shaking her head too. "I really don't know what anyone sees in that ridiculous big tooth-head. He's all teeth and no pants."

I can feel myself getting *really* angry

now. I've been looking forward to this all week, and now they're ruining it. "Be quiet!" I hiss. "I want to hear the chorus."

But they won't clam up.

"*Bite it*? Is that all he can sing about? Being mean? I don't think that's a very good example to be setting for the youngsters of Shark Point," Dad says in his "serious" voice.

"He's not mean!" I protest. "Not really."

"Gulp in ONE BITE, cuz I'm a great white!" screams G-White from the jelly-fishion.

Mom and Dad just look at me.

I'm torn. I just want to listen to the song, but I feel like I have to defend Gregor. He is my hero after all. I want to be like him. Even if the only thing I could gulp with one bite is a minnow. Actually, I couldn't even manage that when I met Marmaduke the Minnow, my new friend. That doesn't matter, I tell myself. I have to convince Mom and Dad that G-White is a good shark now.

I open my mouth to continue the argument, but Mom holds up her fin.

"Not another word, Harry," says Mom. "I think we should turn to another channel; I'm really not happy about you watching this. Great whites shouldn't even be allowed on jellyfishion, the way they frighten communities. It's a disgrace."

"But Gregor isn't like that anymore,

Mom. He hasn't eaten anyone for two years, seven months, and eleven days!"

"No, Harry. I'm sorry," Mom grabs the remote from my fin and flicks the jelly-fishion channel.

"Oh, Hubert."

"Oh, Gloria."

Oh no! It's *Drownton Abbey*! Two terribly fancy crabs are having a terribly fancy conversation, while doing some terribly fancy kissing, in the terribly fancy drawing room of a TERRIBLY TERRIBLE COSTUME DRAMA!

"Mom, it's just an act! Gregor isn't scary. He just pretends to be!"

"Well," Dad says, "he's scaring us by polluting the waves with his awful noise."

I can tell that they're not going to let me see the rest of the performance. The thing I've been waiting for the whole entire week is ruined.

"You two just don't understand!"

I swim up from the chair and swish out of the den, slamming the door behind me. I go straight to my room and throw myself onto the bed.

"It's not fair!" I shout, with a couple of prickly tears in my eyes trying hard to get out. I wipe them away with the tips of my fins. Then I beat my fins on the bed.

Barrap! Barrap! they go as they hit the seaweed blanket.

Hmmm.

Actually, that's not a bad beat.

Barrap, barrap.

Thud. Thud. Swish! goes my tail.

That rhythm's pretty good, I think to myself. Suddenly, I feel a little bit better. Maybe I've discovered a cool new talent. Maybe I'm not so different from G-White after all. I mean, he's a huge great white wrestling, movie, and singing star, and I'm just a little nobody hammerhead, but what if I can rap too?

Barrap! Barrap! go my fins.

Swish. Thud. Thud! goes my tail.

"I'm a hammerrrrrrrrrrrhead. And that's a bit bad actuallyyyyyy," I rap.

It didn't even rhyme.

I try again. A little faster on the bar-raps this time.

"H-h-h-h-hammerhead. I'm kinda blue if you look at me in the right light, and sometimes nearly red."

No, I'm not. I'm never red. That's just really silly.

I need something better that rhymes with hammerhead.

Lots of cool things rhyme with great white. That's why G-White's rap sounded so good. I have to think. . . .

"Hammerhead . . . hammerhead . . . sounds just like jam and sea-bread."

That is clearly the worst rap in the history of the world. Ever.

And then I hear someone laughing.

I look up from the bed, and see Larry, my lantern-fish night-light, and Humphrey, my humming-fish alarm clock. They're both rolling on the floor, clutching their sides and giggling like crazy at my dorky attempts to rap like G-White.

"Stop laughing!" I yell.

Larry looks at me, his lantern flashing on and off as he chuckles. "You mean you weren't trying to be funny?"

"No!"

"Are you sure?" asks Humphrey, buzzing away happily.

"Yes!"

Larry and Humphrey help each other off the floor, both trying—and failing—not to laugh.

"Be quiet, you two!" I shout, pulling the seaweed blanket over my hammer. "I'm trying to sleep."

But I can still hear them giggling

as they swim back to the shelf above my bed. Great. I bet G-White's alarm clock and lamp don't ever laugh at him.

Sometimes it really stinks being a hammerhead shark. Sometimes it's even worse. And then there are days like today, when just about everything goes wrong and it's worse than worse can be. As I drift off to sleep, I hope that some day I'll finally get to meet Gregor the Gnasher. If I met Gregor, he could show me how to wrestle, or act, or rap. . . .

Then no one would laugh at me.

I bet he could teach me stuff that would blow Larry and Humphrey and my mean parents out of the water!

But until then, I'm just going to be a dull hammerhead—that NOTHING COOL RHYMES WITH!

CHAPTER 2

In the morning I can't wait to get out of the house. Even though it's Sunday, and Sundays are usually boring in Shark Point. Mom and Dad don't even notice that I'm not talking to them over breakfast. They seem to have completely forgotten that they upset me last night.

Dad's writing a speech as his breakfast goes cold, and Mom keeps tickling me behind my hammer and calling me her "little starfish." I just stare into my bowl of kelp krispies and bite my lip. I bite it a bit too hard as Mom tickles me again.

"Ouch!" I say.

No one notices.

Great.

I bet this doesn't happen in G-White's house. I bet everyone notices the second he gets mad about something. I leave my bowl on the table to show them how angry I am. But Mom just picks it up and puts it in the dishwasher without saying a thing.

It's like I don't exist!

I grab my jacket and head over to Ralph's. At least he'll be glad to see me.

Ralph lives in a block of coral apartments about five minutes swimming away from our house. But I get there even quicker than usual because:

1. It's Sunday so there's hardly any traffic on the roads.
2. I'm swimming extra fast because . . .
3. I'm still angry about what happened last night and . . .

4. I'm even angrier that at breakfast, Mom and Dad acted as if nothing happened.

Sometimes making a list helps me think more clearly and get my thoughts in order. This list doesn't. When I go over it again in my head, I feel even angrier and swim even faster.

I swish to a halt outside Ralph's bedroom window.

"Ralph!" I call. I wait a bit and the window opens. Ralph's head pokes out and he yawns.

"Morning," he says, rubbing his eyes and sliding slowly out of the window,

still in his pajamas. It isn't like Ralph to be so sleepy. He's usually raring to go in the mornings because he wants to get his breakfast out of my mouth. Pilot fish eat the leftovers from between sharks' teeth, and yes, it is as gross as it sounds. To be honest, I'd rather have a toothbrush, but then how would Ralph eat? So I open my mouth and wait.

Ralph yawns again, and quickly pokes around, pulling out a few half-eaten kelp krispies. He chews them slowly.

"What's up with you?" I ask.

"Late night," he says between little yawns. "I must have watched G-White about a hundred times on rewind. It was awesome, wasn't it?"

I start feeling angry about last night, so I try to change the subject as quickly as I can. "Yeah, awesome. So what should we do today?"

Ralph gives yet another yawn. "Sorry,

Harry. I've got homework to finish before tomorrow. I was supposed to do it last night, but I was too busy watching G-White. Mom says I have to do it today."

Great.

"Why don't you go and see what Joe's doing?" says Ralph, scratching his belly and swimming slowly back up to his bedroom window. "See you at lunchtime, okay?" He disappears inside without even waiting for a reply.

I'm furious.

We always get together on Sunday mornings. But now Ralph can't make it *because he stayed up too late watching G-White.*

I swim away in a huff, darting through town as fast as I can. By the time I get to Joe's family's cave I'm a little bit calmer, but not much.

I ring the bell and through the hanging fronds I see Joe float up to the entrance. He bumps into the wall and looks at me with bleary eyes.

"Yo!" he says slowly, with a yawn.

I can see exactly where this is going. "Up late watching *The Shark Factor,* right?" I ask.

Joe nods and his body changes

from yellow to light green, the color he always goes when he's really, really tired.

"Yeah, it was awesome, wasn't it? We watched it over and over again. Well, I was behind the sofa at the beginning because those explosions were a bit loud, but otherwise it was GREAT!" Joe sticks out his tentacles and scowls, in an

impression of G-White when he was floating on the column of bubbles. "I'm thinking of changing my name to Jel-Fish. What do you think?"

If I say anything, it will just be nasty, so instead I nod and try to put on a convincing smile.

Joe relaxes a few of his tentacles. "Yeah, I think it suits me too."

If I grit my teeth any harder, I think I might break them. "Are you coming out?" I manage to say.

Joe shakes his head. "Sorry, bro, Jel-Fish gotta stay in his crib and help the parental unit with the house."

"You mean your mom wants you to clean your bedroom?" I say.

"Truth."

I can't stay a second longer or I'll explode, so I wave good-bye and swim away in a double . . . no . . . *triple* huff.

It seems I'm the only person in Shark Point not to have seen the jellyfishion event of the year. All because my parents are the uncoolest parents in the ocean. As if it isn't bad enough having a head shaped like a hammer, now everyone will think I'm 100 percent more dorky because I didn't get to see G-White.

I swim down to the park, but it's

empty. Everyone's still in bed then. Great. I swim on.

It seems like the whole town is taking a long time to wake up and get going, even for a Sunday. The stores are deserted and I'm getting more and more bored. I'm getting so bored that I'd even be happy to see Rick Reef and Donny Dogfish, my two least favorite sharks. Even Donny snickering while Rick FLUBBERS my head would be better than this.

My tail is starting to ache and I realize I've been swimming around too fast for too long. I decide to rest for a bit. I'm by my

school now and I can see that the play-grounds are empty, so I swim down to the finball goalposts and lean back against the net.

I wonder what G-White is doing after his performance last night. Is he wandering around his hometown like Billy No-Friends feeling all down in the dumps? Of course he isn't. He's probably in his gold-plated hot spring, scrubbing his back with gold-plated scrubbing brushes while gold-plated pilot fish delicately pick the leftover caviar from between his gold-plated teeth.

Humph. I turn around and bury my hammer in the net.

"It's worse than being dead, being a ham-ham-hammer head," I whisper to myself. "I should've stayed in bed. I'm a ham-ham-hammerhead."

I flex my fins. I want to pound the ground with them.

"What kind of lyrics are they?" someone calls out from behind me.

Huh?

"They're, like, totally the worst lyrics EVAH!"

I flip around and see Cora and Pearl, the dolphin twins. They must have swum up behind me while I was trying out my latest useless rap.

Cora and Pearl strike poses. They look just like G-White's backup singers.

"If you wanna do lyrics right . . . ," says Pearl.

"You gotta sing about love," says Cora, and they high-fin each other.

"You gotta get smoochy-woochy." Pearl blows a kiss at Cora, who takes a picture of her on her SeaPhone.

"You gotta get lovey with the dovey." Cora puckers her lips and flutters her eyelashes as Pearl takes a picture of her. Pretty soon their camera-phones are flashing almost as much as the lights on *The Shark Factor* last night.

I think I'm going to be sick. I start to

swim away, but the camera flashes are following me.

"Don't you want us to help you, Harry?" says Cora as she swims alongside me.

I say nothing. I don't want to be mean. It's not their fault I didn't get to see G-White last night. I just want to be left on my own to sulk.

Pearl starts to rap while Cora drums her fins on her stomach. "Harry wants to sing, but he ain't got a thing. Bring it."

I swim out of the school grounds toward the Point, but the twins don't look like they're going to leave me alone.

They're having far too much fun rapping about me.

"Harry, don't run away—listen to what we say. Word."

Hopefully they'll leave me alone soon. I swim on like crazy, trying to get away from them. But Cora and Pearl swim after me, laughing and singing. I stick my fins in my ears, but I can still hear them.

I'm at the Point now. There's nowhere else to go except the deep ocean. If I just

ignore the twins, maybe they'll go away.

Or maybe they won't. Maybe today is going to be even worse than yesterday!

And then something catches my eye. Out in the dark wall of water beyond the Point I see a huge shadow.

I take my fins out of my ears.

"Don't look so sad; you're really not that bad."

"Yes, he is."

"I know—I just wanted a rhyme."

"Shhh!" I say. "Look!"

I point toward the shadow. It's big and getting bigger. I squint into the darkness.

Oh, man!

It's a great white.

And it's coming this way.

But it's not just *any* great white.
I'd know that shape anywhere.

It's GREGOR!

CHAPTER 3

"It's a great white!" I yell.

But before I can say that I think it's Gregor, the twins start SCREAMING.

"We're under attack! We're under attack!"

CRASH!

That's Cara knocking into my left

hammer as they rush to get away.

"Wait!" I yell. My head is stinging and my stomach feels like a washing machine as I spin around and around. "He's not going to hurt you."

But it's too late. I manage to stop myself spinning and see the twins racing back toward town screaming, "We're all going to die! We're all going to die!"

I look back over my shoulder. Gregor is still moving toward me through the water. But I can't stay and talk to my hero.

I've got to find Pearl and Cora. I've got to stop them.

I try to use my hammer-vision to locate a fast-moving current to ride on. Dolphins and hammerheads are both fast swimmers, but Pearl and Cora have had a good head start and I'm still dizzy from all the spinning.

Unfortunately, it seems that the lazy Sunday feeling of the town has spread to the water, as the currents are all really slow. I'll just have to kick my tail as hard as I can.

My muscles are starting to cramp from all the swimming I've already done this morning. But I can't stop. I need to catch up with the twins. I kick even faster and feel myself surge through the ocean. I'm going almost as fast as Gregor! I can do this! I'm sure I can get to them before they cause any panic.

Or maybe not.

As I reach the main road, I see fish, sharks, and crabs coming out of their houses and stores. Some are still in their pajamas. Some little kids are crying, and their moms and dads are putting their fins around them.

"Have you seen them?" a squid calls to me as I zoom past.

"Seen what?"

"The school of great whites. The twins said they're about to attack Shark Point!"

Oh no! This is worse than I thought.

Panic is spreading through the town. A turtle bus coming in from the Crabton road has clearly tried to turn around and crashed into the side of a supermarket. It looks like all the passengers and the turtle are okay, but the coral wall of the supermarket has a huge hole in it, and loads of bags of piranha puffs are drifting out into the water.

I swim on.

In the distance I catch a glimpse of

Cora and Pearl as they reach Seahorse Square. If they've caused this amount of panic just going up the main road, who knows what's going to happen next!

I kick on, ignoring the pain in my tail and fins and the burning in my gills.

Cora and Pearl disappear around the corner. All I can hear is the buzz of conversation from the fish and sharks in the street. The number-one topic is "Shark alert!"

When I get to Seahorse Square, there's already a crowd gathering around Cora and Pearl. Fish, dolphins, crabs, and sharks. The dolphin twins are outside

the mayor's office, banging on the door.

"What's all this noise about?" a voice shouts from the other side of the square.

Oh no!

It's Dad. He's got his mayor's chain around his neck. He pushes through the crowds toward his office. Mom is swimming behind him and her face looks all concerned. I can see that she's looking for

me and she's really worried. I hold up my fin and wave to her, knowing exactly what's coming next.

Mom catches sight of me and her face lights up. "Angelfish! You're all right!"

"Yes, Mom, I'm fi—pshhhttttthh!"

I'm trying to say that I'm fine, but she

swims across so fast and throws her fins around me so hard that my mouth is buried in her coat.

More and more fish are cramming into the square. Everyone seems terrified. I need to do something.

"I need to do something!" Dad says.

Huh?

He swims up above the crowd, waving his fins around.

"Citizens of Shark Point!"

Everyone ignores him and continues to panic.

"CITIZENS OF SHARK POINT!" Dad yells at the top of his gills.

Everyone still ignores him.

Mom lets me go. "WILL YOU ALL BE QUIET?!" she shouts. Silence falls.

Mom's using "the voice." It's the voice she uses to tell me off when I've been very bad. It's loud and it's scary. I hear a bottom tooting.

I look around, and see Joe blushing as he swims into the square. "Sorry!" he whispers.

He's followed by Ralph, Rick, and Donny.

It seems like the whole town is here. Rick takes a flubbery swipe at my hammer, but I manage to duck out of his way

and float nearer to Mom. He wouldn't dare to now, not when she's using "the voice."

"Citizens of Shark Point," Dad says again, a little calmer now. "We must not panic. We must be calm. We must not worry ourselves unnecessarily!"

"It's all right for you; you're a shark," a turtle calls from the crowd. "It's not you who's going to get eaten, is it?"

The shouting and the panicking start again. An old, ruddy-faced dolphin called Mr. Bottlenose brings Cora and Pearl forward. "Now, tell everyone what you saw, girls."

Cora trembles.

Pearl shakes.

"Well, w-w-w-we didn't really see anything," Cora stutters.

"H-H-H-H-Harry did," Pearl says, pointing at me.

It seems every eye in the square is now looking at me. I can feel my cheeks turning red.

"Oh, look, he's turning pink, just like a girl," Rick snickers to Donny.

Mr. Bottlenose swims up and looks at me. "Did you see great whites, boy?"

"Yes, but only—"

Before I have time to tell them the

rest, Mr. Bottlenose is spinning around, yelling, "It's true! It's true!"

"Um, if we could just calm down a bit," says Dad.

Mr. Bottlenose grabs my fin. "Take us

to them, boy," he bellows. "We've got to see what we're up against!"

With that, twelve strong dolphins come out of the crowd and follow as Mr. Bottlenose leads me back toward the edge of the Point. Mom and Dad swim after us.

"You've got to listen!" I plead, but Mr. Bottlenose waves me aside and swims on determinedly.

Ralph and Joe swim up beside me. "You had any lunch yet?" asks Ralph.

"Is that all you can think about?" I say.

"I'm starving! I hardly had any of

your kelp krispies earlier because I was so tired."

"Don't remind me," I say a bit grumpily. But I don't mind I missed *The Shark Factor* so much anymore, now that I know we're about to see Gregor in the flesh. And hopefully then everyone will calm down. Gregor is a superstar now— he's not going to eat *anyone*.

Eventually we get to the edge of the Point. Mr. Bottlenose pushes me forward. "Where are they, boy? Show us."

I flick on my hammer-vision and scan the dark water ahead. "Mr. Bottlenose, please, it's not—"

"No need to be scared, boy," Mr. Bottlenose interrupts. "Just show us where you saw them and we'll do the rest."

The strong dolphins are rolling up their shirtsleeves and getting ready for trouble.

PING!

My hammer-vision bursts into life and starts giving me information.

Gregor's still here! And he's coming toward us.

PING! Fifty feet and closing.

PING!!! Forty feet and closing.

"What can you sense, boy? Tell us!" Mr. Bottlenose yells.

"It's a great white, all right," I say. "And it's coming this way . . . but, Mr. Bottlenose, you must listen to me, it's only Gre—pshhhtttttthh."

That's Mom, pulling me into her coat again. "Don't worry, my little starfish. I'll protect you!"

"But li—pshhhtttttthh! It's okay, we're not in any da—pshhhtttttthh!"

I give up.

The strong dolphins have all formed a line on the edge of the Point, protecting the crowds of fish and sharks behind them. My hammer-vision is *PINGING* like crazy.

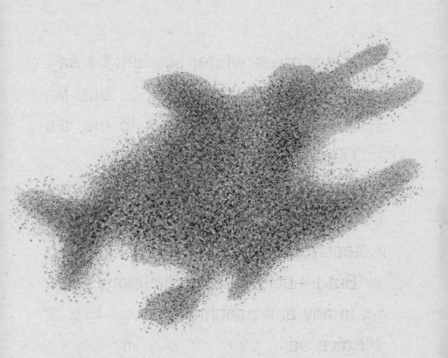

We can all see the shadow coming toward us out of the gloom. It's the biggest shark I've ever seen.

It must be Gregor. But then . . .

"Sea-flowers for sale, sea-flowers!

Who will buy my lover-ly sea-flowers?"

Huh?

Double "huh?"

TRIPLE "HUH?"!

Out of the gloom comes the shark. But it's *not* a great white.

It's a great big basking shark! She's wearing a long floral dress and a floppy fern hat, and carrying a huge bag of flowers. "Oh, who will buy my lover-ly sea-flowers? Bouquet of sea urchins? Vase of coral clusters?" she says.

The citizens of Shark Point aren't panicking anymore—they're laughing.

At me!

The basking shark can't stop grinning
as the relieved townsfish rush up to her
to buy her flowers.

FLUBBER!!!!

Rick boings my rubbery hammerhead

from behind. "Awesome hammer-vision, T-Bone face," he whispers in my jangling ear. "What's going to be next? Giant squids under all our beds?"

A new, horrible list starts writing itself in my mind.

1. I can't rap.
2. I'VE GOT A STUPID HEAD!
3. My hammer-vision isn't working properly anymore.

My hammer-vision was the ONLY cool thing about being a hammerhead. Now everyone thinks it doesn't work.

There are now exactly ZERO cool things about being a hammerhead shark.

ZERO cool things about being ME!

CHAPTER 4

Cora and Pearl aren't talking to me. They blame *me* for the panic *they* caused in town yesterday.

Rick and Donny snicker and whisper every time they swim past me in the school hall.

Joe and Ralph are trying to be nice,

but I can tell they're a little bit embarrassed to be friends with the 'kid who cried great white,' as everyone on the jellyfishion news last night was calling me. You would think that Mom and Dad would be trying to cheer me up, but no. They've been too busy trying to get Dad on jellyfishion so that he can tell everyone what a great mayor he was yesterday.

When I get to my desk in class, I see that someone has drawn a big bunch of flowers on it.

Great.

I'm never gonna live this down.

Luckily, the first lesson after assembly is PE with Mr. Skim, our flying-fish teacher, and there's going to be a cross-seabed swim. At least that gives me a chance to make the other kids remember that I'm a fast shark with a great sense of direction (when my hammer-vision is working properly, that is).

Mr. Skim is waiting for us on the field, doing fin-ups in his shiny track-suit. "Okay," he says, getting up as we file out of the locker rooms. "The route for today's cross-seabed swim is quite simple. From school you take the

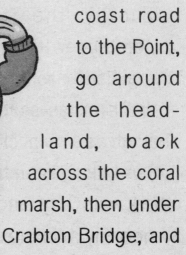

coast road
to the Point,
go around
the head-
land, back
across the coral
marsh, then under
Crabton Bridge, and
back to school. Any questions?"

My stomach sinks as Rick raises a fin. "Mr. Skim, what should we do if we see any vicious, dolphin-eating, urchin-chewing, crab-killing, fish-feasting FLOWER SHARKS on the swim?"

Everyone, including Ralph, thinks this

is hilarious. If the seabed could open up and swallow me right now, I'd be the happiest hammerhead alive.

Mr. Skim smiles but doesn't play along. "Any *serious* questions?"

Rick and Donny are high-finning each other, and Cora and Pearl are typing something on their SeaPhones. Probably putting Rick's joke up on Plaicebook.

Great.

Mr. Skim blows his whistle, and the swim is underway.

I kick away with my tail as fast as I can. Normally I would swim slower to be with Ralph and Joe—they're not as fast as me

and I don't like to leave them behind. But today, I just want to get my hammer down and swim as fast as I can. My face feels waaaaaaay red after Rick's joke, and the faster I go, the cooler the sea water is, taking the heat out of my cheeks.

I get to the Point in record time, just ahead of the leading pack. Rick's a very fast swimmer, but I think he's too busy fooling around with Donny and showing off to the dolphin twins to keep up with me today. I sneak a look behind me, and see him swimming on his back, blowing bubbles out of his gills at Cora and Pearl who are laughing their heads off.

I kick on.

Over the Point and on to . . .

Oh, blubber!

I can't remember which way Mr. Skim wanted us to go. Was it around the headland first, or down across the coral marsh? If Rick and the others see me going back to ask directions, I'll never hear the end of it. "Harry's had another hammer-vision epic fail!" I can almost see their Plaicebook status updates now.

I zoom down onto the coral marsh, convinced that I'm going in the right direction. I kick on and on, determined to get to the finish line first.

The water is getting warmer. I can feel it on my face.

Double blubber!

I should have taken more time to think about the route. It would have been the headland first, before the coral marsh, because from the Point, the coral marsh route will take me straight toward . . .

The shallows.

This is the one place that none of us are allowed to go, except accompanied by an adult. As the spongy coral marsh thins out, the seabed becomes sandy and shallow. The light becomes much brighter, and the water much warmer.

The chances of bumping into human beings, or leggy air-breathers as we call them, are really increased here.

But if I turn around, and go back the way I came, I'm going to be last in the cross-seabed swim.

I *can't* be last.

What should I do?

Then I have an idea. If I continue on, right across the shallows, there's a coral channel that doubles back and comes right out at the Crabton Bridge. If I go as fast as I can, I could use that instead of going around the headland, and still win the race.

Smart!

I swish my tail and start swimming at double speed.

The seabed is leveling out. The water is heating up like a lovely relaxing hot spring, and the sunlight glitters all around. It's a shame we don't get to go to the shallows very often, it's a really beautiful and welcoming place. . . .

PING!

Huh?

My emergency hammer-vision is kicking in at the first sign of danger. Up above me is a huge shadow blocking out the sun. Suddenly, I'm in a shaft of cold water, and I don't know if I'm shivering from the cold or from fear.

Probably both!

The shadow is big and black as it skims through the water. My hammer-vision is *PINGING* off the scale. I slam to a halt. There's only one thing that shadow can be.

A shark.

I listen to hear if it's selling flowers.

Nothing. No sound at all.

A huge shark cutting silently through the water can only be up to one thing.

Hunting.

And a shadow that big can only be from one kind of hunter.

A GREAT WHITE!

Now I'm torn.

Do I want to go on and win the race, or should I go back, get the others, and show them that I *do* know a great white when I see one?

Oh, man . . .

Okay. I can win a race ANYTIME, but this might be my only chance to show them that my hammer-vision *does* work!

I turn around, hurrying out of the shallows and back across the coral marsh.

I'm imagining the twins' Plaicebook updates once I prove to them that my hammer-vision works. . . .

I zoom out of the marsh and slam hard into Ralph and Joe, who are still slow-coaching their way down from the Point to the headland.

"Hey!" says Ralph.

Pop. Pop. Pop. Pop, says Joe's rear. "Watch it!" he manages to yell before his arms and fronds curl up into sea-horse tails in my wake.

"Shark!" I say breathlessly, pointing back over the coral marsh. "Shark!"

"Yeah, right, what's this one selling?

Dolls?" Rick has appeared with Donny behind Ralph and Joe.

"I don't have time to argue—there's a great white shark! A big one—in the shallows!"

Ralph looks puzzled. "What were you doing in the shallows? That's not on the route."

"I took a wrong turn."

Rick and Donny are giggling bubbles into the water. "Hammer-vision gone wrong again?" says Rick.

"If you don't believe me, why don't you come and have a look for yourself?" I press my nose right into Rick's face.

He looks a bit shocked. "All right. Show us."

I lead the way, pulling Ralph by the fin, and feeling Joe cling to my tail with several of his many tentacles.

Rick and Donny follow, but at a safe distance. They're not as brave as they pretend to be.

We burst out of the coral marsh and head up toward the shallows. The weather up above the sea seems to be getting worse. There are lots of clouds now, and the water is full of shadows. It's going to be hard to spot the . . .

But yes—right above us—the *huge* shadow!

"There it is!"

Ralph, Joe, Rick, and Donny look to where I'm pointing.

And that's when the sun comes out from behind the bank of clouds.

And then I see Donny, Rick, and Ralph
start to laugh.

Joe just giggles out of his rear.

Huh?

I look back up.

Oh.

No.

89

In the bright sunlight, the shark is revealed in all its glory.

Its pink glory.

Its plastic glory.

Its girly pink plastic shark-shaped glory.

It's a raft. One of those plastic blow-up things used by the leggy air-breathers to float on the water.

It's not a shark.

And now I'm so uncool, you could fry sea-cucumber fritters on my face.

Ralph stops laughing when he sees my shoulders slump. Then he pokes Joe, who immediately stops tooting.

Rick swims so close to me, I can count the go-faster stripes on his tracksuit. "Nice one, Harry. You can't even tell a great white shark from a raft. Wait until everyone at school hears about this!"

Rick and Donny high-fin, and swim
away laughing.

I can't believe I've been so dopey.
Again!

CHAPTER 5

When school finally finishes, I sneak past the field, darting behind clumps of sea plants. I just want to get away as quickly as possible without being seen. Rick, Donny, Ralph, and Joe are playing finball with some other kids from class. Normally I'd stop and play too.

Not tonight.

Not after the day I've had.

Everywhere I went today, in every class, fish have been pulling my fin about the raft—even Mrs. Shelby. When Mr. Gape, our basking-shark librarian, came in, she said, "Now don't worry, Harry, there's no need to be scared. I know he looks like another type of shark. . . . "

You know you're in trouble when *teachers* are laughing at you.

I slink away from school and the happy sounds of the finballers. Rick has just scored a curling net-ripper and everyone is going crazy cheering. The dolphin twins are singing "Ra ra ra, Rick!" like cheerleaders on the sideline.

Well, that's okay.

I don't need friends. I don't need anyone to play finball with.

I bet G-White doesn't care about friends. Why would he, now he's a famous wrestler, movie star, and rapper?

And one day, I'm gonna be just like that.

H-Hed. That's what I'll call myself. That's a great name for a . . .

Sigh.

Yeah.

It's *totally* awful. I can't even come up with a good rapper's name. I might as well just give up.

When I get home, Mom's bustling around the kitchen making snacks. I hang up my book bag and coat, thinking that at least today can't get any worse.

"Oh, good!" Mom calls out when she sees me. "I need you to go to the newsstand." She goes over to her finbag and takes out some money. "I didn't get a chance to pick up my *True Love Forever* magazine earlier, and it always sells out really quickly. Can you go out and buy me one while I finish my snack?"

Why is it that whenever I think a day can't get any worse, it always does?

Now, hammer-vision-fail-raft-spotter-boy is going to have to swim to the newsstand and ask for a copy of *True Love Forever* magazine. Knowing  my luck, Cora and Pearl will be there, filming it on their SeaPhones to upload straight onto CrewTube.

But if this doesn't go wrong, then something tomorrow is bound to.

So what's the point in fighting it?

I put out my fin for the money.

"Make sure it's this week's though," Mom says. "The one with the bright pink cover and the free Twilight Trout Pout lipstick."

Great.

I swim out of the house and off to the main road, my heart nose-diving with doom.

I can tell everyone's looking at me as I swim slowly along. I've been all over the news for two days now—I'm the laughing stock of Shark Point.

A prawn whizzing by on a

skateboard asks me if I'm on my way to the optician's to get my hammer-vision tested.

I ignore him.

A hermit crab puts his pincers over his head in an arch. "Look out, I'm a great white!" He laughs so hard, his shell falls off.

I ignore him, too. If this goes on much longer, I'll be ignoring all of Shark Point.

Thankfully, there's no one else around when I get to the newsstand, since it's on a quiet side street. The store after the newsstand is the Wet Pet Shop. Usually when I come here, I press my hammer up at the window to look at the kittenfish in their tanks. But today I can't be bothered. I just want to buy the magazine and get the embarrassment over and done with.

The Wet Pet Shop door is locked and there's a big "Gone Fishin" sign hanging on it. No wonder the street is so quiet—if the Wet Pet Shop is closed, there's hardly any reason for anyone to come down here.

Finally, my luck seems to be changing. I'm just about to take the magazine from the newsstand when . . .

Grrrrrrrrrrrrr!

Wow, my stomach is rumbling like crazy. I hadn't even realized I was hungry.

Grrrrrrrrrrrrrrrrrrrrrr!

I don't think it's ever rumbled so loud in my life.

Grrrrrrrrrrrrrrrrrrrrrrrrrrrrrrrr!!!

But hang on a minute, I don't think the low growling, grumbling, rumbling noise is coming from my stomach after all.

PING!

My hammer-vision starts going off.

PING!

PING!!!

"Yeah, right. So what is it this time? A rubber pacifier with teeth?" I say.

PING!

PING!!

PING!!!

I have a look around on the main road, but I can't see anything wrong. It must be COMPLETELY broken. Great. I'm a hammerhead with no hammer-vision.

Annoyed, I glance back the way I came and nearly do a double fin-flip in shock. This time, there *IS* a great white!

It's huge, it looks super mean, and it's hanging above the Wet Pet Shop, staring down at the window. But it's not about to go "Awwwwwwww" at the kittenfish. It's licking its lips and it's

Grrrrrrrrrrrrrring, getting ready to go in for the kill!

I have to do something! I have to say something!

"H-h-h-h-hello. H-h-h-h-h-how are you?"

Yes, I know it's nonsense and I sound like I'm terrified. But that's because I am terrified, and I don't know what else to say.

In the window, the kittenfish are trying to hide under each other.

"Shut it, kid, can't you see I'm busy?" the great white growls. "I'm about to have my snack. Shouldn't you be going home to get yours?"

The great white starts dropping slowly in the water, licking his lips and winding up his tail.

"You don't get your snack from the Wet Pet Shop." My heart starts beating a million times too fast in my chest.

The great white looks at me with his big black eyes.

"Where else am I going to get live kittenfish? I love the way they wriggle as they go down my throat."

The kittenfish start getting more panicky in their tank, swimming around in circles, squeaking and mewing. This just seems to make the great white even more excited. He opens his mouth and gnashes his teeth.

I look around for anyone else who can come and help. But the street is still deserted.

I dart back up to the main road, desperate to tell someone, *anyone*, what's going on. I swim up to a whale and her kids.

"Quick! Down there! There's a great white!" I gasp.

The whale just smiles and pats me on the head. "Yes, of course there is, dear. I don't think you're going to get us with that one again. Nice try though!"

"But—"

The whale just swims on, with her kids finning their noses at me.

Oh no!

I dodge some turtle-cars and go up to an octopus who is looking in a jeweller's window at eight-holed engagement rings.

"Help!" I shout, shaking him by the tentacle. "There's a great white at the Wet Pet Shop! He's about to eat the kittenfish!"

The octopus turns and looks at me. "Forget it, kid. I heard all about your great white prank on the jellyfishion." He blows ink in my face and goes back to looking in the window.

I dart up and down the street, looking

for someone else to tell. I'm near the
side street when I hear . . .

CRASH!

It's coming from the Wet Pet Shop.

The great white must be starting his attack!

CRASH!

I start swimming faster. I can't leave the kittenfish to him. I have to do something to stop them from becoming the great white's snack—even if it means I end up becoming his dessert!

CHAPTER 6

I know that this really isn't the best time to make a list. But a list of things that make me happy will make me feel less scared. As the great white winds himself up to smash into the Wet Pet Shop door again, I start listing like crazy in my head.

1. **Kelp krispies**. I like them! I'm so close to the great white now. I can see a piece of seaweed trapped between his teeth.

2. **Ralph**. He's great. I like him! I'm so close to the great white now. I can see a tattoo on his dorsal fin saying: **FIGHT 4 THE RIGHT TO BITE**.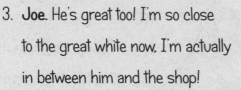

3. **Joe**. He's great too! I'm so close to the great white now. I'm actually in between him and the shop!

4. **And Mom and Dad**. I love them, too! I really, really love them!

I've reached the end of my list.

"STOP!" I shout as loudly and as scarily as I can.

The great white is all coiled up, ready to smash into the door of the Wet Pet Shop for a final time, as the hinges are just about to give way. He pauses for a moment. He stares at me with his huge, black, mean-looking eyes.

"You again? What did I tell you a minute ago, kid? Get out of the way or you're in big trouble."

"Kittenfish? What kind of cowardly shark eats kittenfish? Well, obviously a coward with all the bravery of a dead haddock." I cannot believe what just came out of my mouth. Now I'm dessert for sure.

"What did you say?" growls the great white.

Oh well, if I'm going to be a great white's dessert I suppose I've got nothing left to lose. "Are you deaf as well as a coward? Or just *out to lunch*?"

Oh. MY. COD!

"GRRRRRRRRRRRRRRRRRRRRRRRR-RRRRRRRRRRRRRRRRRRRRR!!!!!"

The great white lets his wound-up tail go and leaps straight at me.

But that's exactly what I wanted. "Catch me if you can!" I yell, and I'm off too.

Zooooooooooooooooooooooooom!

PING!!! PING!!!

I know, hammer-vision! I know!

I shoot off toward the main road, knowing the great white will follow.

My hammer-vision clicks automatically to ESCAPE MODE. I hope this time it doesn't let me down.

ZOOOOM! I shoot round the corner. A

turtle taxi screeches to a halt as I shoot on to the road.

"Watch where you're going!" screams the taxi driver, waving his flipper with anger.

"GREAT WHITE!" I scream as I dart over him.

"Just you wait 'til I tell your dad the mayor about this!" the driver shouts. "You're going to be grounded for . . . for . . . for . . . "

The great white zooms out of the side street after me, and the turtle's jaw drops down in shock. "For . . . for . . . for . . . It's a GREAT WHITE!"

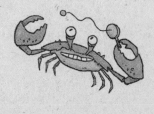

"That's what I *said*!" I cry as I shoot down the street with the great white snapping at my tail. As I go, faces change from smiles and laughter to total terror as they see what's snarling away behind me.

Fish dive into store doorways, squids slide under turtles. Outside

Guppy's Grocery Store boxes of sea fruit get smashed into the air by my hammer-head, and telephone poles get knocked over by the wild flapping of the great white's huge tail.

I can tell from the currents in the water that he's gaining on me.

"I'm gonna chew you up and spit you out, boy!" the great white shouts.

"You've got to catch me first!" I yell behind me.

My hammer-vision escape mode is pinging away, warning me of any obstacles. A turtle bus from Crabton pulls out in front of me and I squeeze under it. The great white has to go over.

I swim off the street out toward the Point. A school of minnows is returning from a class outing. I skirt around the side of the group. The great white is too big to swerve that quickly and he ploughs on straight ahead. Luckily, the teacher, an old hermit crab with little glasses and a knitted sweater, has pushed all the young fish aside, and the great white just sails through.

I'm kicking and kicking, turning this way and that. But the great white is still gaining on me. I'm trying to think of ways to shake him off.

I turn a sick full 180 half-fin, and barrel

into a reverse tail-endy. This sends the great white flying over my head, and suddenly I'm heading away from the Point in the opposite direction.

I'm starting to get tired now, so I know I won't be able to keep this up for long.

"Come here!" the great white bellows, finally managing to change direction and follow me again.

I don't know what I'm going to do. I've managed to lead the great white away from town, but now what?

PING!

My hammer-vision is looking

waaaaaaaaaaaaaaay ahead. It zooms the school playground right into view.

I can see Rick and the others still playing finball, and my hammer-vision super senses send me faint sounds of Cora and Pearl, still cheerleading.

I can't go right, because that will take me over the coral marsh.

I can't go left, because that will take me out into the wide ocean.

I can't go back, because the great white will just eat me!

I've got to go on, but that means I'm going to lead the great white . . . *straight to my friends!*

"Great white!" I scream as the playground gets closer and closer.

I can see Rick about to take one of his fancy-pants free kicks with the finball. Everyone else is concentrating on that, rather than me and the great white shooting toward them at top speed!

"GREAT WHITE!" I yell again at the top of my voice.

"Pipe down, Harry! Can't you see I'm concentrating?" Rick calls over his shoulder. He continues lining up the ball.

We're almost there. I can feel the vibrations in the water as the great white's jaws chomp after my tail. I can

feel the hot, hungry breath blowing from his gills.

What am I going to do?

Rick takes a float back. He's ready to kick.

Ralph is floating between the goal posts, wearing goalkeeping gloves on his fins. He's focusing hard on Rick, getting ready to try and save the ball.

"OUCH!"

The great white is nipping at my flukes.

"I can almost taste you, kid!" he snarls.

Ralph looks over Rick's head—straight at me and the great white.

"Great white!" he yells.
"You won't fool me with lame-o tricks like your goofy friend," Rick sneers.
"Great white!" calls Joe. *"Pop pop pop pop pop pop,"* calls his rear.

"Oh, zip it!" Rick yells.

"Ra ra ra," the dolphin twins sing. "Ra ra raaaaggghhhhh!" the dolphin twins scream as they turn to look at what Ralph and Joe are looking at. Me—being chased by a great big great white.

Rick starts swishing his tail angrily. "It's my free kick. Stop trying to ruin it!"

"Rick!" yells Donny, pointing wildly with his fin. "LOOK!"

And finally Rick *does* look.

And then he just about breaks the sea-speed record for hiding behind twin dolphins with your rear tooting like a motorboat!

"GREAT WHITE!" he screams as he flies behind Pearl and Cora.

"I know!" I scream back as I skim low across the field. And then an idea pings into my head even louder than my hammer-vision. I start waving my fins madly at Ralph in the goal.

"Ralph! Get out the way!" I yell.

Ralph dives to the left, covering his head with his fins.

I've got just one chance for my plan to work. I head straight for the goal, kicking as hard and as fast as I can. The great white's hot gill-breath is sending shivers up my spine.

The goal posts come up really fast. I hold out my fins and curl my whole body into a sharky body-knot. I grab the top of the post with my fin and hope that my speed will be enough to carry me around. It is. I spin around the post, up over the crossbar, and as I come around I flick out both flukes of my tail as hard as I can.

CRACK!!!

The great white's nose connects perfectly with my tail-flick. The nose is where great whites keep all their most sensitive hunting sensors and delicate S.H.A.R.K.D.A.R. equipment. It's also the most vulnerable place on a great white's body. If you're ever facing a great white, hit him as hard as you can on the nose.

BOIIIIIIIIIIIIINNNNNNNNNNGG!

The great white's eyes snap shut and his body goes limp. He's traveling so fast that his whole body flies forward, knocking me aside as he shoots right into the goal.

ONE-ZERO HARRY!

The great white is completely uncon-
scious as he floats in the water, but he
won't be for long. I swim up, unhook the

net from the crossbar, and drape the net over him. Then, grabbing the net in my teeth, I swim around and around until he is totally tied up.

Done!

"Yaaaaaaaaaaaaaaaay!" cry the dolphin twins.

"Yesssssssssssssssssssssssssss!" cry Ralph and Joe.

"Has it gone yet?" whimpers Rick, still hiding behind Pearl and Cora.

And then it seems like the whole town is crowding on to the finball field, coming to see what's happened. At the head of the crowd are Mom and Dad.

Mom throws herself at me and gives me a massive hug. "Starfish! You've saved us all!"

For the first time ever, I'm not embarrassed by Mom calling me starfish. But that's probably because everyone is pointing at the great white trapped in the net and cheering like crazy.

Cheering ME!

Dad high-fins me, then raises my fin like I'm a champion wrestler. "I'm so proud of you, son," he says with a smile.

Ralph, Joe, Cora, Pearl, and even Donny the Dogfish are pushing their way through the crowd toward me. Ralph and

Joe can't stop smiling. Cora and Pearl are snapping away with the cameras on their SeaPhones. Donny is clapping and cheering! In the background I can see

Rick getting off the seabed and dusting himself off with his fins. He doesn't look happy at the attention I'm getting.

But I don't care. It's AWESOME.

"Harry's hammer-vision saved us all!" Dad shouts, and from the clapping and cheering it seems like the whole town agrees.

I can't believe it. Just this morning I was so down in the dumps that I wanted the seabed to swallow me whole. Now I'm on top of the ocean!

As everyone gathers around me, high-finning me and slapping me on the back, I realize something so shocking, it makes my goggly eyes spin. Ever since I can remember, I've wanted to be a great white, but I'm a hammerhead who *outwitted* a great white. It's not just G-White who has the shark factor.

I've got BUCKETS FULL of it!

A Fin-tastic
Finish

CHAPTER 1

"Daaaaaaaaaaaaaaaaaaaaaaaaaaaaaad! Get your fin-pit OUT OF MY FACE!!!!!!!"

I'm trying to see past my dad's stinky fin-pit down into the Olimpet Stadium, where the final race of the Underwater Olimpets is about to take place. And where Turbo Tex, the fastest shark in the ocean, is about to try to win his fifth gold medal of the games!

I squeeze my hammer head under Dad's pit so I can look down into the massive whalebone-and-coral arena.

All of Shark Point is here. The arena is filled with color and noise. Some of the sharkletes are limbering up by the track but one is missing. Yes! I haven't missed Tex's entrance.

"Harry!" Dad squirms as I push past him. "Y-y-your dorsal is tickling me!"

Dad—Hugo Hammer, or Mayor Hugo Hammer, as he's known to the rest of Shark Point—starts giggling and twisting. He bumps into my mom and the huge box of Weedpops she's bought for me goes flying up above our heads. Me, Ralph (my pilot-fish pal), and Joe (my jellyfish friend) watch, openmouthed, as it gets caught in the currents caused by the crowd and floats away.

"I was really looking forward to picking those out from between your teeth!" Ralph whines. (Ralph's a pilot fish, which means he eats his food from out of sharks' mouths. My mouth in particular.)

I shush Ralph with my fin and try to spot my new hero.

I still like my old hero, Gregor the Gnasher, but he's retired from wrestling and making films and gone to work as an ambassador for the UN (the Underwater Nations). So he's hardly on jellyfishion anymore— only the news. And who watches the news?

But since the Olimpets started and tiger shark Turbo Tex came along, I haven't really cared. Tex is great because . . .

1. Tiger sharks are fast and totally scary. Their stripes make them super camouflaged in the water, so they're the best hunters.

2. Turbo Tex is the fastest, scariest, and strongest of the group. The best sharklete in the whole ocean. Scarier than a mom who's just found out you've shoved everything under your bed

instead of cleaning 'properly.' Yes. THAT scary.

3. Tex does the TIGER TURBO (more on this in a minute and you'll see exactly how cool it is).

4. He's so fast he's already won the 100 and 800 fathoms in these Olimpet Games. Probably because he doesn't have a goofy hammery head to slow him down like me.

Basically, Turbo Tex is so cool you could use him to make icebergs.

The crowd goes wild as the announcer clears his throat loudly and starts speaking.

"And now, in lane six, the winner of gold medals in the 100 and 800 fathoms, the gold medalist and new world-record holder in the long dive and triple pike, it's the one, the only, the very stripy Turbo Tex!"

I stretch my hammer head as far as it will go to see Tex coming down the tunnel onto the swimming track. He's being pulled on a huge clamshell by three dolphin girls. He waves to the crowd, then, with a wink, he swims off the shell. He's going to throw his signature move—THE TIGER TURBO! (See number 4 in my list.)

BOooOM! Tex disappears in an explosion of bubbles as he begins to barrel roll like an out-of-control washing machine. He spins on the spot with precision power as a white whirlpool of water builds around him, then—*wowsers*! The bubbles from the whirlpool come together to form a giant *T*. Tex stops dead in front of it with a huge toothy smile on his pointy, stripy face.

The crowd goes even wilder. Mom and Dad are out of their seats, cheering like crazy. I can't imagine how excited

everyone will be if Tex actually wins the turtle-hurdles.

Tex takes his place on the track and fits his fins into the starting blocks. The turtle-hurdles look huge but the other sharks in the race seem to be more interested in Tex. Their eyes bulge as Tex flexes his tail and sets his nose at the right angle to get the best kick for the first bend.

Bang! The bullet mackerel is fired by the starting octopus. The race is on!

Tex is first out of the blocks, kicking away with a whoosh of his tail.

The bramble shark in the next lane

is blinded by the bubbles and shoots off sideways. The crowd gasps as he crashes into a group of schoolsquids on a visit to the stadium with their teacher. The squids are sent flying in all directions.

The bramble shark bounces off a row of seats and Tex is waaaaaaay in the lead as he jumps the first turtle-hurdle.

Tex powers around the first bend. In second place, a sleek cookiecutter shark kicks and kicks, trying to make up the distance to Tex. But he's nowhere near as powerful as the speeding tiger.

Wham! Tex takes the next turtle and turns his head sideways so that the electric-eel photographers can get the best picture of him with their cameras.

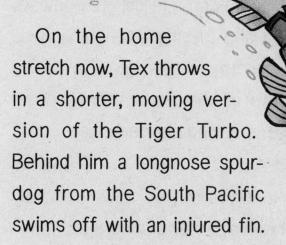

On the home stretch now, Tex throws in a shorter, moving version of the Tiger Turbo. Behind him a longnose spurdog from the South Pacific swims off with an injured fin.

Tex, now knowing that he can't be beaten, jumps the next turtle upside down and now he's swimming with only one fin!

At the last corner, the three other sharks still in the race—the cookiecutter, a velvet dogfish, and a gulper shark—can only fight not to come in last. Tex powers on, kicking and turning and whirring so that the current moves into the crowd and flutters all the flags and banners! The noise is incredible because:

1. Dad is screaming!
2. Mom is screaming!
3. Ralph is screaming!
4. I'm screaming!
5. Joe is hiding from all the screaming!

As Tex crosses the finish line, there are a million electric-eel flashes and a roar that threatens to send a tsunami across the surface of the ocean.

"Mayor coming through! Mayor coming through!" Dad shouts as he starts shouldering his way through the crowd, not even bothering to wait for the other sharks to finish the race. I quickly swim after him. Dad flashes his mayor's ID card at the security crabs guarding the

track and they shuffle apart to let us pass.

Usually I hate it that Dad is Mayor of Shark Point. He normally wears silly bow ties and vests, and he makes terrible jokes whenever he's giving a speech. But right now, being the mayor's son seems like the coolest thing in the world because Dad is heading straight for Turbo Tex!

Tex is waving to the crowd, and has his five medals hanging around his neck. Dad pushes up to him, takes him by the fin, and pumps it up and down about a thousand times.

"Mr. Turbo, can I say that was the most exciting race I've ever seen," he gushes.

Tex looks down at Dad. "Yes, you can say it." Tex winks at me then turns back to Dad. "Go on."

Dad frowns, not really getting the joke, so I nudge him in the side. "Say it again, Dad."

"Oh. That was the most excit—"

Tex laughs and slaps Dad on the

153

shoulder with a big, meaty fin. "Only joking, dude. You the mayor of this town?"

Dad nods. "I certainly am, and can I just say how honored—"

Tex slaps Dad on the shoulder and winks at me again. "I guess this little fella must be your boy, then?"

Dad nods again. "Yes, that's Harry, and as I was saying—"

Tex goes to slap Dad on the shoulder yet again, but Dad has learned his lesson and backs off. Tex sees that I'm holding out my autograph book and a cuttlefish pen. He reaches down and signs his name right across two pages.

"I'm way too big to fit on one page, kid!" he says with a grin.

Coolest. Thing. EVER!

My smile's so big it's threatening to split my hammer in two.

"Get your phone, Mr. Mayor," Tex tells Dad.

Nodding and trying hard not to open his mouth again, Dad reaches for his SeaBerry.

Tex spins me around to face Dad and flops his fin around me. "Smile wide, kid!"

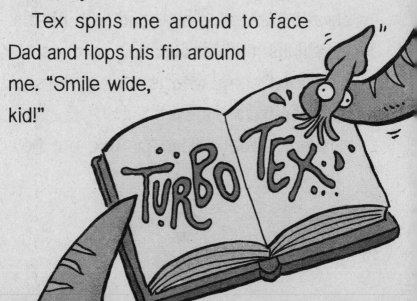

But before I can open my mouth . . .
FLUBBBBBBBBBBBBBEEEEERRRRRR!!!!

The world shakes and my eyes start rattling in my head. I hear Rick Reef snickering as the camera on Dad's SeaBerry flashes.

When my dopey rubbery head finally stops vibrating, Rick Reef and Donny Dogfish come into focus. Rick is hold-ing his belly and laughing hard. He's always flubbering my head with his fin. He thinks it's hilarious, and so does his sidekick Donny, who is wiping tears of laughter from his eyes.

I look about wildly for Tex, but he's

already swimming off with his fins draped around the dolphin girls.

"Oh," says Dad, looking at his phone.

"Did you get the picture?" I ask, swimming over to take a look.

"Well . . . sort of . . ."

My heart sinks as I look at the screen.

 Rick flubbered me just before Dad took the picture. Tex is smiling and waving—*Next to a hammerhead-shaped blur*!!!!

Outside the Olimpet Stadium, I kick empty Weedpop boxes along the ground as the crowd streams around us. Ralph and Joe are doing everything they can to cheer me up, but it isn't working. All I can think about is my ridiculous flubbery head, and Rick ruining what was probably the only chance I'll ever have to get my picture taken with a superstar.

I kick another empty box, and huff like a sea cow.

Boing!!!!

For a moment, I think that Rick's come back and flubbered my head again. But when I look up I see that I've bashed into someone. Someone wearing a bright red cap and scarf and a whalebone woggle.

"Look where you're going, boy!" a voice booms.

My heart sinks. The voice belongs to Drago Dogfish, leader of the Shark

Point Cub Pack, and dad of Rick's side-kick Donny!

"*Attennnnnnnnnnnnnshun!*" bellows Drago, straightening his scarf and pushing back his cap with a pointy fin. "Have you seen Donny? He should be busy getting ready for camp tomorrow—as should all of you!"

In the excitement over Turbo

Tex, I'd forgotten we're off to Cub Camp tomorrow. If my heart sinks any further, I'm going to have to dig it out of the seabed.

Drago glares at us. Joe starts to *pop, pop, pop* from his backside, and Ralph tries to hide in my mouth.

"I just asked you a question!" Drago barks. "Tell me—what are you supposed to do when someone asks you a question?"

"We have to answer, sir," I say.

Drago shakes his head.

I look at Ralph and Joe. They look as baffled as me.

"You don't just have to answer. You have to give *the very best answer possible!*" Drago says. Then he stares at me. "Go on."

I look at him blankly. "What?"

"Give me your *very best answer possible.*"

I point back to the stadium with one end of my hammer. "I—er—think Donny's still in there with Rick, sir."

I'm not sure if that's the very best answer possible but thankfully Drago starts to smile. "I see," he says. "I bet he's checking out the equipment and preparing for *all the awesome races and sporting challenges* I've got planned for you boys at camp."

No, I think to myself. He's probably up to no-good with Rick, looking for poor, unsuspecting hammerheads to flubber just when they're having the *most important photographs of their lives taken!*

But of course I don't say it.

"Ah, that Donny, he's a chip off the old block," Drago says. "Always thinking ahead. *Always doing his best.* Not like the rest of you, slouching home when you could still be in the Olimpet Stadium learning things. You'll never amount to anything with that kind of attitude. You won't be winners like my boy Donny. You'll be losers! Is that what you want? *No!* No, it isn't! Life is about pushing yourself to the limit, not tooting from your bottom, hiding behind someone else's teeth, or failing to look where you're going! Do I make myself clear?"

Me, Ralph, and Joe nod.

Well, Joe toots again, but he tries nodding too.

"Okay! I expect to see you three

bright and early tomorrow morning. I have plans for you all. *Plans!*"

Drago pulls himself up into a salute, straightens his scarf again, then swims off toward the stadium.

I slump to the seabed. "Just when

you think the day can't get any worse, it does," I say.

Ralph and Joe agree. Not one of us is looking forward to two days of being yelled at to *do our best* by Drago Dogfish.

I look up, hoping to see something—anything—to make me feel better. But all I see is a huge picture of Turbo Tex looking down at me with enormous eyes and sparkly teeth.

If only I was a supreme sharklete like Tex. Then everyone would love me and Drago wouldn't shout at me and Rick wouldn't dare flubber my head.

But the fact is, I'm just a boyshark with a dopey head shaped like a hammer. Tex is a winner and I'm a loser.

In fact, the only Olimpet gold medal I could win right now is the one for Most Flubbery Head in the World!

CHAPTER 2

I snap one eye open. It's still dark.

I snap my other eye open. Now half of the room is a little brighter but the other half is still very gloomy.

That's when I realize that one end of my hammer is still under the pillow and the other is flopped over the side of my seabed.

I look around the room. Humphrey, my humming-fish alarm clock, is still fast asleep. If I've woken up before he's gone off I *must* be nervous. I'd already set him earlier than usual so I had time to get ready for camp.

At the thought of camp, I swim straight out of bed. If I want to be a sharklete like Turbo Tex I need to start training pronto. Plus I really need to get in shape for whatever Drago has planned. I know I've waited till the last minute—but a quick workout has got to be better than nothing.

I think back to the sharkletes limbering up and stretching in the Olimpet

Stadium before their race. I try warming up my tail.

It stays cold.

I start stretching out my fins.

They stay stiff.

I begin rolling my hammer.

It wobbles and flubbers all by itself.

Great!

Drago's voice drifts back into my mind. "You won't be winners like my boy Donny! You'll be losers! Is that what you want? *No!* No, it isn't! Life is about pushing yourself to the limit!"

Well, if pushing yourself to the limit is what's needed, then it's time to *push!*

1. I start with sit-ups. Hup! Hup! Hup! (Ouch! Ouch! Ouch!)

2. Move on to dorsal jumps. Flap! Flap! Flap! (Ache! Ache! Ache!)

3. Start fifty fin presses. I manage two. (Twinge! Twinge!)

4. Roll for a sequence of hammer jerks. (Flub! Flub! Flubber!)

5. Leap high for a toothy jaw snarkle.

CRAAAAAAAASSSSSSSSSHHHHH!!!!
My out-of-control flubbery hammer bounces into Lenny the Lantern Fish,

171

who immediately floods the room with light and . . .

HMMMMMMMMMMMMMM!!!

HMMMMMMMMMMMMMMMMMM!!!

Humphrey wakes up in panic and starts his alarm humming on the loudest possible setting!

My next bit of exercise is chasing them both around the room, trying to turn Lenny off and stop Humphrey from humming so loudly he wakes Mom and Dad.

When I finally catch them, I see that Humphrey is not happy at all.

"It's my job to wake everyone up!" he moans. "I'm a humming-fish alarm

clock, that's what I do!" He turns and glares at Lenny. "Are you trying to put me out of a job?"

Then Lenny gets angry too. "It wasn't my fault!" He points at me. "It was him! He flubbered me sideways and I panicked!"

Lenny and Humphrey glare at me.

"That's what you have to do if you want to be a winner," I say. "Push yourself to the limit!"

"Any more of that," says Humphrey,

"and we'll push you down a whirlpool!"

"Sorry!" I say, as I have another idea. "Look, I need your help. I'm trying to get fit for Cub Camp today. I need you two to be turtle-hurdles."

They both look at me like I've lost my mind. But they don't understand. Turbo Tex didn't win the Olimpet turtle-hurdles (on his back, with just the one fin) without a lot of practice.

I place Humphrey and Lenny equal distances apart in my bedroom: Humphrey on my seaweed blanket and Lenny next to my flaptop, and then . . .

Whoosh, I'm off! Zooming around the

room, kicking with my tail, and . . .

Leap!!! I'm over Humphrey!

Zoom!!! I'm coming around my seabed!

Leap!!! I'm over Lenny!!!

ZOOOM!!! And I'm coming around again!

This is fin-tastic! At last something is going right!!!

LEAP!!! And I'm . . .

SMASHING!!! into Mom as she floats through the door with a tray of breakfast . . .

I hit her fins so hard that the tray spins out of control, turning the bowl of prawn flakes out all over my seabed.

Breakfast *in* bed has become breakfast *on* bed.

I look at Mom.

Mom looks at me.

She is not happy.

Neither are Lenny and Humphrey, who have also been splattered with prawn flakes.

"I've got breakfast all over my lantern,"

Lenny grumbles as he swims back to his shelf.

"I'm a humming-fish alarm clock, not a humming-fish hurdle!" Humphrey hisses as he swims back to my bedside table.

"Harry! You silly boy!" Mom says. "There isn't any time for playing. You've got to get ready for camp."

"I'm not playing, I'm training!" I reply angrily.

Hmmm—I bet Turbo Tex doesn't have to put up with this kind of thing.

Mom is unusually quiet as we swim down to the bus for camp. Normally, when we swim anywhere, she likes singing one of her terrible songs, but her mouth is shut tight, and her hammer is looking straight ahead. Perhaps she still hasn't forgiven me for wrecking breakfast.

Loads of other parents and kids are at the whalebus by the time we get there. The bus is filling up. The whale underneath is yawning and looking really bored. Ralph and Joe are aboard already and waving at me from one of the windows.

I turn to Mom to say good-bye, and that's when the most embarrassing thing that has ever happened to anyone ever in the history of seaworld happens.

She starts to cry!

Then she pulls me close and wraps her fins around me—in front of everyone!

"I can't believe my little starfish is going away for two whole days!" she sobs. Then she eases her grip on me and turns around. "You will look after him, won't you, Drago?"

I turn bright pink from the top of my hammer to the flukes of my tail. I peek one end of my hammer out from under Mom's fin. Drago is floating at the entrance to the whalebus with his clipboard, ticking off names. Right next to him, just about to burst out laughing, are Donny and Rick.

"Don't worry, Mrs. Hammer, your little starfish will be safe with me," says Drago as he checks off my name.

"Moooooooooooommmmm! Let go!" I whisper, hoping that no one else is looking. But of course they are. When I glance up at the bus I see noses and eyes and sonar pods pressed against every window.

"Ah, mommy's little baby," Rick sneers gleefully. "Mommy's little itty baby who should be put in a carriage."

I can even see a smile creeping across Drago's mouth as he shoos Rick and Donny onto the whalebus. "Enough of that, boys. I won't stand for any non-sense. Not on my watch."

I finally manage to wriggle out of Mom's clutches just as she tries to plant a slobbery kiss on my hammer. I drag my backpack onto my back and dart on to the bus, as Mom waves and cries.

Things don't get any better on the bus. Mom held on to me for so long, there are hardly any seats left. Rick and Donny are at the back, making faces out of the window. Ralph and Joe are about halfway down. I start to make my way along the aisle towards them, but

a fin grabs my shoulder and spins me around.

"Not so fast, boy!" booms Drago. "Your mom's made me promise to keep a special eye on you, so that's exactly what I'm going to do!"

I want a freak sea current to whoosh onto the bus and wash me straight back off again.

Drago sits me down in the seat next to him, and makes a great show of putting on my seat belt.

From the back I can hear Donny and Rick start to sing, "Baby, baby, stick your head in gravy . . . "

A ripple of giggles fills up the whalebus. I bury my hammer in my fins and start making a list of how bad camp is going to be to try to drown out the song.

1. Trapped for two whole days with Rick and Donny.

"Baby, baby . . ."

2. Made to look like a complete and utter loser by Drago.

"Stick your head . . ."

3. Everyone laughing behind their fins at me (to be honest this has started already. I can see them now).

"In gravy!"

4. And this song following me wherever I go!

See what I mean?

I sink into the seat and cover my ears.

But then I see something that makes me sit up straighter than a ship's mast.

A tiger shark is getting on the bus. A tiger shark just like Turbo Tex!

Well, he's only a kidshark like me, but he's a *real* tiger shark! He swims up the bus, not making eye contact with anyone (waaaay cool), carrying a stripy backpack that matches the stripes down his side.

"This is Tony," Drago calls out, making a note on his clipboard. "His family has just moved to Shark Point and he'll be joining us at camp." Drago turns to

Tony. "I'm expecting *great* things from you, boy!"

Tony swims slowly past Drago. The other kids stop singing and watch. I can hear Rick whistling through his teeth tunelessly because he's no longer the center of attention.

Suddenly I have a plan. A great, magnificent and awesome plan.

1. I'll make friends with Tony Tiger.
2. I'll get him to teach me how to become a supreme sharklete.
3. Then I'll be faster than the others and win *all* the races.
4. This will shut Rick and Donny up for good!
5. And I'll have the best time *ever!*

CHAPTER 3

The Sea-cub Camp is located many leagues away in the Frondy Forest. After a few hours, we head into the sea cliffs. The whalebus starts driving through narrow passages and ravines, kicking its flukes slowly so it doesn't dislodge any rocks. Slimy strands of seaweed form a gloomy tunnel of brown above us.

But I can hardly concentrate on the journey because I can't take my eyes off Tony Tiger. He doesn't look at me, but then he doesn't look at anyone. Far too cool for that, I guess.

When we get to the camp, it's a relief to be out in the light, but the forest of huge brown and black weeds still surrounds us on all sides.

Drago gets us out of the bus. I try to float as close as I can to Tony, but he doesn't seem to notice me at all. I wonder if he heard Rick and Donny's song about me.

A piercing shriek rings out, making us all jump. Drago is wearing a whalebone whistle around his neck and he's blowing it so hard it's making his eyes even gogglier than mine.

We all quickly get into line, floating as straight as we can. Drago stops blowing his whistle and starts swimming up and down in front of us.

"You know what time it is," he says. "And I know what time it is."

We all look at him blankly.

"Five past twelve?" Joe says nervously.

Drago blows his whistle loudly. *"No! No! No!* It's time for the Sea-cub Motto!"

We all pull ourselves up as straight as we can and use our loudest voices. "I promise that I will do my best," we say.

"No! No! No! No! No!" Drago yells. "I've changed the words. From now on, our motto is: I promise that I won't do my best—"

We all stare at him.

"I promise that I will do *better than my very most all-time best!*" Drago bellows.

Hmmm, it doesn't flow quite as smoothly as the original motto—especially when we try it.

"I . . . promise . . . very . . . than . . . better . . . most . . . best . . . all-time . . . ," we stammer, apart from Tiger Kid, who says nothing. He really is Cool. As. Ice.

Drago sighs. "Okay, enough of that. It's time to *get down to business! The business of being the best!*" He starts swimming around and around in a circle. "This camp will push you *to the limit.* It will test you *to the max.*" He swims

faster and faster. I'm starting to get dizzy just watching him. "It will . . . it will . . . " Drago stops swimming and crashes into Donny.

"Dad!" Donny says, looking embarrassed.

"Sorry, son. Got hit by a—er—freak current." Drago quickly straightens his cap. "Anyway, as I was about to say, by the time we get to the *competition* tomorrow you're all going to be working together as a team." He looks at us and narrows his eyes. "And remember, there is no *I in team!*"

"Now time for the first exercise,"

Drago continues. "Putting your tents up. The last one to get his done will have to drop and give me fifty!"

None of us dare ask him fifty what.

Luckily, I'm one of the first to get my tent up. This is mainly because I don't need to borrow a hammer to knock in the tent pegs. I just use the side of my head.

I look around. Rick and Donny are sword-fighting with their tent poles. Ralph is trying to find

WHAM!
WHAM!
WHAM!

Joe . . . who is hiding from an octokid swinging six hammers at once.

Tony Tiger's trying to get his tent up, but doesn't seem to be doing a good job of it. I bet it's because he's too cool to ever go camping. Then I realize that this is a perfect opportunity to put my plan into action.

"Hi, Tony? I'm Harry," I say, swimming over. "Do you need some help?"

Tony looks away.

Man, I must be so uncool he doesn't even want to be seen talking to me in case he loses his seacred.

I decide to try again

and swim around to face Tony. "My head's pretty good at putting up tents. Look . . . "

I bang in a couple of pegs to show him, and get the back end of his tent up. Tony just floats there, his cool stripes glistening in the light. He even looks fast standing still.

I just look like a hammer with a tail.

I try a joke. "Are those go-faster stripes?" I say, pointing at his side.

Tony just looks at me like I'm something your fin might slide in.

Great.

I swim around quickly putting up Tony's

tent, not bothering to say anything more.

"Time's up!" Drago yells, just as I finish.

Rick is next to his tent, but Donny is nowhere to be seen. Then I notice his tail sticking out under the tent flap. He's holding it up from the inside to make it look like they've finished. Cheats!

Ralph and Joe are still trying to get their final tent peg in. Joe has turned bright red from the effort.

"Okay. Ralph and Joe, drop and give me fifty!" Drago bellows.

"Fifty what?" asks Joe.

"Tooty-pops," sniggers Rick, flicking

the flap of his tent to cover Donny's tail.

"*Fin-presses!*" yells Drago.

Ralph and Joe begin . . .

Press, press, press.

Pop, pop, poppity-pop.

When Ralph and Joe have finally finished, Drago leads us all into the Frondy

Forest. The weed trunks are huge and dark, and wide leaves sweep backward and forward in the slow currents. Dark little fish dart in the hollows and strange rustles in the undergrowth make us look this way and that.

It's all a bit creepy.

Drago leads us into another, smaller clearing. "Okay, you bunch, it's time for the real work to begin! Welcome to *the best obstacle course the underwater world has ever seen!*"

As my eyes adjust to the brightness, I see what he's talking about and my stomach does several flips.

The obstacle course is a huge collection of spinning wheels, tiny holes, sticky nets, and water-powered whirring tentacles. We all stand openmouthed as Drago takes us through each piece of equipment.

"Cubs, your first test is to see if you can get around the course without being spun out of the wheel, stuck in

THE BEST OBSTACLE COURSE
THE UNDERWATER WORLD HAS EVER SEEN!

a hole, tangled in the nets, or captured by the tentacles."

We all look at each other in shocked silence.

Drago clicks his stopwatch and starts sending us off one at a time. I'm in the middle of the pack—in front of

Tony, but just behind Rick and Donny.

"Go on, Donny, show 'em how it's done!" shouts Drago as he sends his son off, with Rick following fifteen seconds later.

Then it's my turn. I look back at Tony. Maybe if I can get through the course in a good time, he won't think I'm such a hammery rubberhead and he'll want to be my friend. I was silly thinking that putting up the tent would impress him. He'll be much more impressed if I can show him some sharklete skills.

It all goes well at first. I zip through the nets, avoid the tentacles, and slip through the small holes in the rocks. I'm doing so well, I'm catching up with Rick and Donny. I really hope Tony is watching.

I kick away from the rocks and head towards the spinning wheel. It looks like the paddle from a sunken leggy air-breather's paddle boat. Strands of seaweed are stuck to its white wooden slats. They whip around as it turns on the current.

Donny has ducked below the wheel to avoid it. Luckily for him, Drago doesn't notice. He's too busy clicking his stopwatch as he sends Tony off. Rick dives between two slats and makes it to the center of the wheel. He hangs on to the hub with a fin as he tries to get the timing right to dart through the slats on the other side.

As I get closer he looks at me and smirks.

I ignore him—it's not Rick I'm interested in. I sneak a look back at Tony as I dive towards the wheel. Rick kicks, narrowly making it out between the slats as it spins around and around.

This is when I realize it was a mistake ignoring Rick. He wasn't just waiting for the right time to swim out between the whirring slats, he was laying a trap for me!

Rick has pulled a long strand of sea-weed into the center of the wheel and looped it around. And now, instead of being a good place to hang on to while I wait for the wheel to rotate, it's all slippery! As I desperately try to hang on to the hub, I slide straight off, bounce into the slats and get tangled in the seaweed fronds hanging there.

Upside down!

I go around and around and around and around and around (I'm gonna be sick!) and around and around and around (I am sick!) and around and around and around. I see Tony slipping easily into

the wheel and out the other side. He completely ignores my embarrassed wave through the cloud of prawn-flakes I had for breakfast. Once the wheel has stopped, it takes three hours for a very unhappy Drago to untangle me from the seaweed.

By that time, everyone else is back

at camp, and I can hear them all singing. ("Sick, sick, Harry's been sick! The wheel turned him around and his breakfast flew out!")

Really—could this camp get any worse?

CHAPTER 4

As soon as I get back to camp I go and hide in my tent until the singing stops. Ralph and Joe ask if I want to come and play finball, but I ignore them. I just want to be alone. But then I smell clamburgers and hotfrogs on the currents washing through my tent and my stomach groans. I undo the tent flap and swim to where everyone is sitting on rafts of pink sea-sponge, around a small whirl-pool.

I spot Ralph and Joe over by Drago, cooking hotfrogs in a handy volcanic vent.

Nothing cheers a shark up more than an approaching meal, so I should be happy, but:

1. No one's talking to me. Mainly, I think, because they don't want to laugh in my face.

2. I can't interrupt Ralph and Joe while they're cooking hotfrogs without getting told off by Drago.

209

3. I catch sight of myself in a passing mirrorfish and I see that I'm still slightly green from my time on the wheel.

4. This makes me feel fed up.

5. Very fed up.

6. Totally fed up.

I could go on, but maybe I should try again to make friends with Tony? I scan the cubs gathered around the whirlpool.

Tony is sitting on a sea-pillow with Rick and Donny.

7. I'm now totally FED UP!!!!!

How can I ever learn to be a great sharklete like Turbo Tex now that Tony is friends with my arch-flubberer?

I turn on my tail and gloomily begin to swim back towards my tent, but Drago spots me.

"And where do you think you're going, Harry?" he shouts.

I stop and shrug. "Dunno, sir."

"Well, how about I tell you? You're going to make up for messing up the obstacle course by becoming our waiter for the night." Drago hands me a tray of clamburgers. "Off you go."

I take the tray and start handing out clamburgers. Rick and Donny take two each and try to flubber my head, but I manage to duck away. When I've finally served everyone, all that's left for me to eat are two empty clamburger buns and half a hotfrog.

I sit on my own at the back of the circle and chew unhappily on my food. Ralph swims over.

"Any food between your teeth?" he asks.

I shake my head glumly. There's not enough for me, let alone my swimming toothbrush!

"Listen up, everyone," Drago says once we've all finished eating. He's sitting closest to the whirlpool and his head is lit up by a couple of lantern fish. The current in the water is making his scarf float around his face like the creepy weeds in the forest. "It's time for a ghost story," he whispers.

Everyone sits for-
ward excitedly,
except me. I
couldn't care
less.

"I want
to tell you
a tale. A tale of a whale. A tale of doom
and a sharp harpoon! Of a moonless
night and a terrible fright, and a whaley
ghost who's coming here soon!" Drago
looks at us all, his face deadly serious.
"It was a hundred years ago, I'll have
you all know, when Jonah the whale was
blown by a gale, out here to the fronds,

to the backs of beyonds, where even leggy air-breathers won't sail!"

I have to admit that I'm starting to get interested in the story. I float a little closer on my sea-sponge.

Drago continues. "Jonah was cold and alone, shivering to the bone, too far from the shore, when he heard the ship roar. A ship of the dead, floating over his head, the captain a ghost, with rotten eyes!"

I move even closer. The dark water around the whirlpool seems to be closing in. I see Donny's fin reaching out to hold Rick's. Rick holds on for a moment, then realizes what he's doing and slaps it away. Donny starts hugging himself instead.

Drago's voice gets lower and whisperier. "Jonah tried to hide, but he was caught by the tide. He was flung on the beach, and the dead started to screech. The dead captain began a-stabbing, under the light of the moon, with his fearsome harpoon!"

Pop pop pop pop pop poppity pop!

I turn to look at Joe. But for once it wasn't his bottom popping—it was the squidkid, Sammy, floating next to him.

Drago starts drifting over our heads.

216

POP!
POP!
POP!

The lantern fishes are now behind him, making him look like a big black shadow. "And now it is said, that this whale who is dead, swims through the dark, seeking fishes and sharks, to feast on with glee, for breakfast, lunch, *and* dinner! *ARRRRRRRGG-GGGHHHHHH!!!!*"

At this point, the lantern fish go out and everyone screams! Even me!

Drago laughs. "Lights on, boys!"

But nothing happens.

217

"Lantern fish!" Drago shouts. "I said lights on."

"We are on!" one of the lanterns calls back.

"I'm sorry," Sammy Squid whimpers. "I couldn't help it."

Suddenly I realize what's happened. Sammy has got so scared that he's let out an ink explosion and it's blocking out all the light!

Drago starts swimming around. "Everyone, shake your tails and clear the ink."

We all do as we're told. As the ink clears, I see Sammy's tentacles totally

caught up with Joe's jellyfish legs. It's like they both tried to hug each other to pieces.

The others rush to untangle Sammy and Joe, but I hold back. Not because I don't want to help, but because I've just been struck by *the best idea ever*!

I can feel my goggly hammerhead eyes growing wider and wider as I realize how brilliant it is. If I play this right:

1. Everyone will stop singing dopey songs about me.
2. I'll be friends with them all again and
3. I'll be a supreme sharklete just like *Turbo Tex*!

CHAPTER 5

Drago has sent us all to bed with the order to "*Dream the dreams of winners!*"

Ralph and Joe are in my tent, going on about the midnight snack they've been planning for ages. They're so excited about it I haven't had a chance to mention my own plan.

"Do we have to stay up until midnight?" asks Joe. "That's way past my bedtime."

"A midnight snack doesn't have to happen at midnight, fishbrains," says Ralph, eyeing the pile of sweets Joe is pulling out of his backpack. "It can be held at any time!"

"Then why is it called a midnight snack?" Joe uses several tentacles to lay out the sweets in neat rows in front of him.

"Because . . . because . . ." Ralph scratches his chin with his fin and thinks. But the sight of all the sweets is obviously too distracting for him. "Oh, I dunno! Who cares?! What have we got?"

Joe finishes arranging the sweets. "Okay," he says, floating back to admire his handiwork. "We've got Kit-Katfishes, Double Shipwreckers, Sealion Bars, Maltweedsers, and a huuuuuuge bag of Seasick 'n' Mix."

"Got any Tangfishsticks?" Ralph says hopefully. "I love picking them out from between Harry's teeth."

"Listen," I say, but Ralph's way too busy gazing at the sweets to pay me any attention.

Joe reaches inside his backpack, and pulls out a brightly colored bag of Tangfishsticks. "Here you go."

"I need to tell you something," I try again.

Ralph grabs the bag, opens it, and shoves it in my face. "Start eating, Harry! I want to get to work!"

I push the bag away. "I haven't got time for a midnight snack!"

"I thought it could be at any time?" says Joe, flashing yellow and purple, like he always does when he's confused. "I don't understand!"

"Just eat a few, Harry," Ralph says. "It won't take long!"

"No, there's something I need to do," I say, brushing past the sweets and heading for the tent flap. "Something way more important than a midnight snack."

They look at me blankly.

"What could be more important than a midnight snack?" Ralph says, his eyes wide.

"Come with me, and you'll see," I reply.

"Can I bring the Tangfishsticks?" asks Ralph.

"No!" I hiss, as I open the flap. "Follow me. And keep your voices down."

Outside, the camp is quiet and mostly dark. The lantern fish have gone out and the only light is coming from the moon reflecting on the ocean above.

"D-d-do we have to go?" Joe starts trembling and his jellyfish body flashes red for danger. "It's too dark and scary!"

I shush him with my fin and swim on.

Suddenly I hear a loud rustling. I spin my goggle eyes wildly.

"Ralph!" I whisper crossly. "I told you not to bring the Tangfishsticks!"

Ralph looks embarrassed and puts the bag back in his pocket.

We swim on through the silent camp, and eventually reach the tent I want. I float up close to it.

"Sammy? Sammy?" I whisper. "It's me, Harry. Are you awake?"

I hear the zip of a sleeping bag being undone inside the tent.

"Well, I am now!"

The flap opens and Sammy Squid sticks out a tentacle, followed by a pair of sleepy eyes. "What do you want?"

"Yes," says Ralph, looking at me, "what do we want?"

"Sammy," I say, ignoring Ralph, "I want you to spray some stripes down my side in ink. I want to look like Turbo Tex. Can you do it?"

"Yes and no," says Sammy.

"I was less confused when we were talking about midnight snacks not being at midnight," Joe mutters. "What do you mean, yes and no?"

"Yes, I can do it, but no, I can't do it now," says Sammy, rubbing his eyes.

I stare at him. "Why not?"

"I can't spray ink unless I'm scared," he replies. "It's a defense mechanism. I need to feel threatened."

I open my mouth and show Sammy my hunter's teeth.

Nothing happens—apart from Ralph trying to dive in for a quick snack.

"Sorry, Harry, but you're just not

229

scary," Sammy says with a grin. "Not even a little bit."

Great—my plan is falling to pieces because I'm not scary enough to frighten a kid squid. I look around, trying to think. The camp is dark and silent, the currents cold and creepy. In the distance, the leaves of the Frondy Forest move lazily in the water like beckoning fingers. It's very, very spooky.

Yes! Got it!

"Okay . . . I have another idea," I say. "What if I told you a ghost story like Drago's?"

"No thanks!" says Sammy, backing into the tent. "One was bad enough!"

"Please, Sammy!" I grab the bag of Tangfishsticks from Ralph's pocket and hold them out to Sammy. "You can have these if you say yes."

"No . . . mmmmmmph! He . . . mmmmmmph! Can't . . . mmmmmph!" Ralph splutters as I put my fin over his mouth to shut him up. I wave the bag in front of Sammy with my other fin at the same time.

"The whole bag?" Sammy says, coming forward again.

"Yes. And all the Double Shipwreckers and Maltweedsers we have back in our tent, too."

I'm having to hold Ralph down now. He's not happy at all.

Sammy nods. "Okay, I'll do it."

"Great!" I say. "Just make sure you get tiger stripes down both sides of me, right?"

Sammy nods, and curls his rear end under his head so it's right in my face.

The things I have to do to save my reputation!

"Right . . . okay . . . ," I start. But my mind is completely blank. I don't know any ghost stories! I look around wildly but I can't think of anything. I'm just going to have to make a story up on the spot. It can't be that difficult, can it?

I screw up my eyes and lower my voice to a whisper like Drago. "Here is a tale about a sea ghost, which will scare you so much, you won't want to eat your lunch, or even . . . prawn toast!"

Bit of a shaky start, but not too bad. I glance at Sammy. He's looking completely calm. Ralph has a face like a grumpy granddad walrus chewing a spine fish,

and Joe is a peaceful shade of blue.

Okay, time to step it up a bit. "It's a terrible story, about a squidboy called . . . er . . . Rory, who was from somewhere . . . near to . . . ummm . . . Tanglemory?"

I look at the others. Joe is still blue, but Sammy is starting to tremble. Yes, it's working!

"He liked to go out, at night all—ummm—about. To the ship graveyard—even though it was hard . . . to get there, because his—er—navigation skills were full of hair."

I frown. I never realized making stuff up could be so difficult!

But Sammy is starting to really shake

now. He's obviously terrified! I'd better carry on. "So, the night of the fright, he went there and—ummm—right, there was a figure in white. Was it a sheet? No—ummm—not quite. Rory did swim away as fast as a . . . umm . . . very fast thing." I growl my best sharky growl. "And he never went near there again!"

Sammy is shaking so much he's vibrating the tent. He's scared out of his tentacles!

Except . . .

1. Sammy isn't terrified. (Not even a little bit.)
2. Sammy is trying not to laugh. (And he's about to fail.)

3. As I finish he can't hold it any longer. (Here he goes.)

4. He starts to laugh, and soon he can't stop. ("Hahahahahahahahaha!!!")

5. Out comes the ink from his rear. (Pffffffffffffffffftttttt!!!)

6. But instead of a stream, it's a spray. (Oh *no*!!)

7. And as he laughs more, it covers me. (Stooooooooooop!!!)

8. Too late. I'm not striped like a tiger shark at all. *I'm covered in spots!*

CHAPTER 6

When I wake up the next morning, the first thing I do is check my skin to see if the spots have faded. I can't believe my goggly eyes. The spots look even worse in the daylight. Instead of looking like a really cool tiger shark, I look like a hammer teen with pimples!

"Come on, you lazy bunch!" I hear Drago shouting from outside. "Sleeping's for losers and waking's for winners! It's time to do some warming up."

I don't need warming up, I need washing down. I rub at the spots with my hammer. But no matter how hard I rub, they just won't fade. Squid ink is EVIL!

I sigh and swim outside. Drago takes one look at me and throws his fins up in panic.

"Okay, everyone—back away from Harry!" He rushes towards me. "I've never seen such a bad case of seasles

in my life! Get yourself back to bed while I call an ambuwhale."

"I don't need an ambuwhale, sir," I say. "I don't have seasles."

"Don't have seasles?" Drago bellows. "Then what in ocean's name do you have?" He eyes me suspiciously. I can't tell him the truth—that would be way too embarrassing. But I have to tell him something. So I tell him a bit of the truth.

"It's a squid fart, sir."

Drago looks as if his eyes are going to burst out of his head. "A what?"

"A squid fart. I made Sammy laugh and he tooted all over me. With ink."

All of the cubs start roaring with laughter. I'll never live this down.

Ever.

Everyone's still laughing at breakfast. Keeping my eyes down, I carry my bowl of prawn-flakes to the very end of the canteen tent and begin to eat. I'm halfway through the bowl before I realize that, completely by accident, I've sat down next to Tony. He's looking straight ahead, ignoring me.

"Okay, Tony?"

As usual, he says nothing. But at least

he isn't laughing. That's something, I suppose.

The first activity after breakfast is volcanic vent surfing. We've each been given a rubber safety suit to protect us from the heat. The others are moaning about having to wear them, but as far as I'm concerned it's a total win. At least with my suit on no one can see my spots!

Drago takes us to a clearing in the middle of the Frondy Forest. A cliff face stretches up before us. About halfway down, a huge stream of bubbling water gushes out of a volcanic vent. It travels

241

along straight for a little, then it's joined by the stream from another vent and goes into a *huge* downhill, twisting and turning and even pulling up into a loop the loop. I've been volcanic vent surfing with my dad before and it's *totally awesome*.

"All right," Drago says as soon as we're ready. "It's time to surf the fear! It's time to feel the heat! It's time to—it's time to . . . I want you to ride the jets of hot water from the vents."

Rick and Donny go first, and are pretty quick. Tony goes second, but he obviously has a bit of bad luck and skims off course (the trick is keeping your whole body inside the current).

I decide to have another try. Tucking my fins close to my body, I barrel roll down the stream, picking up speed, then use my hammer to hook Tony's tail,

swing him round and put him back on course!

I finish just behind him. I grin and go for a high fin.

But my fin is left dangling in empty water. Tony has completely ignored me again!

Ralph swims over. "I dunno why you're bothering. He obviously doesn't want anything to do with you."

Ralph might have a point. My plan to impress Tony hasn't exactly worked as I hoped it would.

Soon it's time for lunch. Drago leads us into the Frondy Forest. "So, cubs, you've all had fun vent surfing, yes?"

We all nod.

"And I bet you've worked up an appetite for lunch, right?"

Everyone nods even harder. Ralph looks at my mouth, fins his tummy, and nods thirty-seven times.

"Well, there's no such thing as a free lunch out here in the wild," Drago says. "No more clamburgers and hotfrogs for you. You're going to have to find your own food. Are you with me?"

We all stop nodding and start groaning. But Drago isn't listening. "You have one hour to come back with the best meal ever! *Go!!!*"

We went.

We came back.

I have:

1. Three bent sea carrots. (Ick.)

2. Half a dog-eared sea cucumber. (Double ick.)

3. Two crab apples. (Quadruple ick, times ten.)

4. Some lobster milk I've collected in my hat. (Ewwww.)

Ralph has three brown, knobbly things that could be tide-ginger or could be sea-cow patties. He isn't sure. Joe was too scared to go into the Frondy Forest alone, so he's been relying on us to bring him back his lunch.

"Actually, I don't think I'm hungry anymore," he says as soon as he sees our offerings.

"I don't think I'll ever be hungry again," I say, sniffing the could-be-tide-ginger-could-be-cow-patty.

Drago starts swimming up and down in front of us. "Okay, now you've had your lunch," he says as I pour the sour lobster milk away, "it's time for the grand finale of this camp. But first, I need to put you into teams. I want

247

Team Fearless to be scared of nothing, Team Awesome to be the *best*, Team Amazing to stop at nothing to *win*, Team Invincible to be *unbeatable*, Team Incredible to *blow our minds*, and Team Supreme to come *out on top* whatever happens!"

I'm not sure how all six teams can be the winner, but Drago is on such a roll I decide not to interrupt him. Drago puts me in Team Supreme along with:

1. Ralph (not bad, I suppose)
2. Joe (could be worse)
3. Donny (and so it is worse)

4. Rick (yup, worse as worse can be)

5. Tony (shall I give it one last try with him?)

Drago puffs his dogfish chest out, and swims between the teams. "This is the ultimate challenge. The one that will stretch you all to the limit."

My mind is racing. What's it going to be this time?

"I've put you in teams because this isn't something you can do alone."

Oh, I hope it's not rock swimming. I hate rock swimming, and Joe has no jelly for heights.

"This will push you," Drago continues.

"This will make you work together, and this will *make* or *break* you as a *team!!!*"

Pop pop pop pop!

(That's not Joe, that's *me!*)

Drago waits for a second. We all stare at him, open-mouthed. What is it going to be?

"You're going to swim a relay race!"

Oh.

Silence. From. Everyone.

Is that all? A relay race? The way Drago was going on, you'd think we were going to be scaling the north trench of Deep Everest!

Ah well, at least Rick won't be able to make me look like a goofball in a relay race.

Drago fires a bullet mackerel, just like the starter in the Olimpet Stadium. The first fish speed away and the race is on!

We've each got to do one lap of the camp swimming track. Joe is first for Team Supreme. His tentacles twirl behind him like streamers and he's carrying the baton in his teeth. Ralph and I cheer him on. Rick and Donny don't seem to be that impressed at being on a team with us. Tony is floating on his own. I can't wait to see him race. I bet he'll be super fast.

"Look at him," Rick sneers as Joe falls behind teams Invincible and Amazing. "He's so slow he couldn't overtake a sea snail."

"Zip it, Rick," I say. "He's doing his best."

"Yeah, but the problem is, his best is awful," Rick says, squaring up to me. "Or have you *spotted* some skills in your friend that I haven't *spotted*?"

Donny points at my ink spots and giggles.

"At least he's trying," I say.

Rick just fins his nose at me and turns away. I look at Tony, but he's not even watching the race.

Drago is looking at his stopwatch as the teams come round the final bend. Ralph gets into position, and holds out

his fin for the baton from Joe. By the time Joe passes it to him he's in fourth place.

Ralph swims off and Joe hangs, deflated, on the fence.

I try to concentrate on the race and not on Donny, who has now got a pencil and is trying to join the dots on my dorsal. Ralph zooms round the track. Pilot fish are used to keeping up with much faster species like sharks, so he's really speedy. Ralph pushes as fast as his little tail will allow. As he swims into the home stretch, we've moved up a place to third!

Donny takes the baton from Ralph and the third lap begins.

"Make sure you don't drop that baton when you give it to me!" Rick shouts. "Or I'll give you a biting you won't forget!"

"Wow, great way to support your teammate," I hiss at Rick.

Rick glares at me. "I don't care about this dopey team. All I care about is getting the fastest individual lap and the medal that comes with it."

Before I can say anything, Rick moves out onto the track to wait for Donny. As Rick stretches out his fin for the baton, Donny comes around in second!

Lap four begins.

Rick zooms off with all the sleek skill of a reef shark. He's soon gaining on the bull shark from Team Invincible who's in first place.

Even I'm impressed—but it doesn't stop me wishing that Rick was a nicer shark to everyone around him.

Rick pulls alongside the bull shark on the back stretch. He flicks his tail effortlessly, nose down. *Kick, kick, kick.*

As they take the last bend, I get into place. Rick comes around in the lead. My heart starts to pound. We might actually have a chance of winning this!

I wait, my fin out, watching as Rick gets closer and closer. I kick away, knowing I'm going to have to match his speed as he reaches for me . . .

Closer! Closer! *Closer! Closer!*

The baton is almost in my grasp, and then Rick hisses at me through his sharp, gritted teeth. "The fastest lap is mine. *Mine!*"

And he drops the baton just as I reach for it! It slips through my fin, looking like it was me who dropped it!

The baton spins down. As the other cubs speed away, they stir up the silt at the bottom of the track, turning the water cloudy. The baton disappears from view.

Quickly, I flick on my hammer-vision and direct it toward the seabed.

PING!

I sense the baton! It's three yards away.

I turn and dive down.

PING!

One yard.

PING!

Fifty yards.

Boing!

The baton bashes into my nose and I grab for it wildly. Grasping it tight, I do a fast 180-degree horizontal tail-kick and push off as hard as I can.

But I'm in last place.

GRRRRRRRRRRRRRRRRRR!!!!!

I am *so angry* at Rick. All he wants to do is spoil things for everyone. Well, Rick, you're *not* going to spoil this race for me. Camp has been a total disaster. I've been laughed at, had dorky songs sung about me, been ignored by Tony, and covered in *squid farts*!

Well, no *more*!!

I kick and kick and kick. With each wave of my tail I imagine the water spreading squid-fart ink all over Rick's sneery smile.

Wave. Waft! Wave. Waft! Wave. Waft! Wave. Waft!

Hahahahahahaha!

It's working! I'm *going faster*!!!!!

I pass Team Fearless into fifth place!

I kick and kick on, moving the baton to my teeth for extra fluid-dynamic sleekness.

I pass Team Incredible into fourth place!

On and on, just two laps to go. My tail

is beginning to hurt but I keep going. The lobster from Team Awesome is flagging and I pass him easily into third place!

One lap to go.

Wave. I picture Rick's smug face being splattered with ink.

I power past the blue-fin tuna from Team Amazing and I'm in second.

There's just the super-fast dolphin of Team Invincible left on the home stretch. I can see Tony getting into position. This is your last chance, I think. If you don't want to be my friend after the lap I've just swum, you're not worth being friends with!

I kick deeper and harder than I ever have in my life. I overtake the dolphin into first place and hold the baton out to Tony.

Tony the tiger shark.

The same breed as the fastest, bestest sharklete in the sea. We. Have. This. Race. Won!

I hand the baton over and Tony is away!

"Go on, Tony! Swim it! Leave 'em for

fish food!" I scream as I clatter into Ralph and Joe, who've swum over to catch me.

Then something happens that I wasn't expecting at all.

Tony doesn't swim very fast.

Huh?

I mean—yeah, he's okay—but there's no coordination. His fins aren't in sequence with his tail at all. He's all over the place.

He does his best, but by the time he comes back around we're in third place.

We *haven't* won the race.

I don't believe it.

Tony swims in, puffing hard. He hands the baton to Joe and swims off without saying a word.

It's the official Medal Ceremony and I'm officially sulking. Camp has been terrible. I haven't made friends with Tony and I haven't done well in a single event. All I've done is been teased and cheated and covered in spots!

Drago has made us all form a circle. He swims into the middle of it and blows his whistle loudly. I know he's got lots of medals to give out. But none of them are for me. I close my eyes and start singing loudly in my head. Maybe if I don't see or hear any of the others winning I won't feel so bad.

"And the winner of—" Drago begins.

La la la la la la la!

"And next up it's—"

La la la la la la la!

"And this year's Best Newcomer is—Tony Tiger!"

Whoops. I forgot to sing. I open one eye and watch Tony collect his medal. He doesn't look very happy about it.

"But, Dad, Tony was the only newcomer," Donny whines.

"Exactly," says Drago. "So he must be the best." He turns back to the rest of us. "And now the medals for the winning team in the relay race."

LA LA LA LA LA LA LA LA LA LA LA LA LA LA LA LA LA LA!

I shut my eyes tight and keep singing away in my head, louder and louder for what feels like forever.

LA LA LA LA LA LA LA LA LA LA LA LA LA LA LA LA LA LA!

Suddenly I feel someone nudging my side. I open my eyes and see Joe and Ralph grinning at me.

"Go on," Ralph says, pointing a fin towards Drago.

Drago is holding out a medal—to me. And he's smiling—at me.

"What's happened?" I whisper to Ralph.

"You've won Fastest Lap in the Relay," Ralph says with a grin.

"What?!" I turn to Joe. "Have I fallen asleep?" I whisper to him.

Joe looks at me like I'm fishbrained. "No. Why?"

I start pinching myself with my fin.

"What are you doing?" Ralph says.

"Checking I'm not dreaming." I pinch myself even harder. "Ouch!" But Drago is still there, holding a medal out to me.

I swim over to him and everyone cheers. Well, everyone apart from Rick and Donny, who are looking really, really, really annoyed.

"Well done, young Harry!" Drago says as he hangs the medal round my neck.

"That was one of the *best, fastest laps I have ever seen in all my years as an olimpet coach*—er, I mean, sea-cub leader."

I swim back to Ralph and Joe, still in shock.

"Okay, cubs, I'm going to see if the

whalebus is ready," Drago calls. "Go and get your tents and bags."

As soon as he's gone, Rick swims over to me.

"There's no way you could have beaten me," he hisses. "I'm a reef shark. I'm one of the fastest sharks in the whalebus."

"You're a cheater," a voice says behind me. A voice I don't recognize. I turn round and see Tony.

"What did you say?" Rick snarls.

Tony's face starts turning pink. "You're a cheater," he says again. "I saw you drop the baton on purpose

when you were supposed to hand it to Harry."

I open my mouth to say something, but I'm so shocked, nothing comes out.

"That's how I know he can't have been faster than me," Rick says. "That's exactly why I dropped it—so that he wouldn't beat me!"

"You dropped the baton on purpose?" We all jump at the sound of Drago's voice. He's swum up right behind us and he's looking really mad.

"I—er—well—I . . . " Rick splutters.

"You and Donny are sitting near me on the bus so I can teach you all about the importance of teamwork—*all the way home!*"

"Dad!" Donny whines.

"B-but—" Rick splutters.

"No buts!" Drago says. "Come on, cubs, let's get going."

As everyone swims off, I turn back to Tony. "Hey, thanks for standing up for me with Rick."

Tony's face turns even pinker. He looks really

embarrassed. "That's okay. I should have said something sooner—when I saw him drop the baton, but . . . " He looks away.

"Are you all right?" I say.

Tony nods. "I'm terrible at talking when I don't know anyone. I get really shy. I think people are going to make fun of me so I just stay quiet."

I stare at him. "Really? I thought you didn't like me because—because I'm a hammerhead."

"No way!" Tony says, and he starts to grin. "I think you're ace. And your lap was awesome! I wish I could swim as fast as you."

273

I feel like I'm dreaming all over again.

Tony looks at me. "D-do you want to sit next to me on the bus?"

I must have looked really shocked, because Tony's eyes drop. "It's okay if you don't want to. Don't worry. Bad idea. Sorry."

"No!" I say quickly. "I'd love to sit next to you."

This is totally awesome!

"So you want to be friends?" I say, just to check I'm not imagining it.

Tony nods. "Yes, please."

I swim up for a high fin and this time Tony high-fins me right back!

The bus is packed and we're all inside. I sit next to Tony in the backseats right behind Ralph and Joe. Rick and Donny are up at the front with Drago. He's giving them a long talk about the "*seven hundred* ways to be the *best team player ever.*"

What a fin-tastic end to the camp!

And then I realize that I've achieved everything in my plan.

1. I'm friends with Tony the Tiger. Check!
2. I'm the fastest sharklete in the sea-cubs. Check!

3. Rick and Donny are sitting in complete silence next to Drago. Check! Check! Check!

4. Things don't get much better than this!

THE END

Splash Dance

CHAPTER 1

"*Moooooooooooooooooooooooooooom!* Stop it! It's breakfast time. I want to eat my breakfast. I want to enjoy my breakfast. I don't want to talk about exams! I want to concentrate on breakfast. Are you trying to give me fin-digestion before I even start eating?"

I don't think Mom is listening. She's swimming around the kitchen, preparing breakfast on autopilot—slooooooooooooow autopilot. There are kelp krispies popping and crackling in a bowl as they turn soggy (and kelp krispies are awful when they're mushy). And she hasn't even put the crab Pop-Tarts in the toaster yet! All she's interested in doing is going on and on about the Quay Stage 2 exams I have to take next month at school.

"Well, Harry, I know studying isn't your favorite pastime," Mom says for the third time as she swims right past the Pop-Tarts, "but it really is important . . ."

In my head I'm yawning. It's a BIG yawn. Not as big as the hungry hole in my tummy, but it's close.

Dad is no help at all. He's got his hammer head stuck in today's *Seaweed Times*, scanning the pages to see if there's anything about him. Dad's Mayor of Shark Point, and usually there's a picture of him in the paper, opening a new building, or kissing a newspawn, or standing next to an important visitor from another reef. He likes to cut the stories out and put them up on the wall of

his office. Today he doesn't seem to have found anything about himself. This always makes him grumpy.

"Dad," I say, "could you pass my kelp krispies, ple—?"

"Not one picture!" Dad slaps a fin against the paper. "I had a dozen photos taken yesterday and not a single one has made it into the paper. It's like I don't exist!" Dad does like to exaggerate when he gets upset. I've got to do something RIGHT NOW, so that:

1. Mom stops talking about exams.
2. Dad stops talking about himself.

282

3. My breakfast moves from the counter to my mouth before the rumbling in my tummy causes a seaquake!

And then I see it.

As Dad grumpily holds up the newspaper, I see an ad for the new Fintendo SeaWii-DS on the back.

Oh, WOW!

All the hunger is pushed from my tummy as I fin up close to the back page. Dad is still huffing and muttering behind it, but I don't

care. I'm too busy looking at the ad for the ultra-new fin-held game console, with SeaWii-DS graphics and Super Snapper Races 8. And it's out today.

I WANT ONE!!!!

"Now, about this studying . . . ," Mom says, finally putting the crab tarts in the toaster.

But I'm not listening, I'm reading all the mouthwatering specs in the ad:

1. SeaWii-DS Screen!
2. Depth-Charge Slider!
3. Circle Pad Canalog Control!

4. WiFi-sh Communication!

5. TONS OF OTHER GREAT THINGS THAT I DON'T REALLY UNDERSTAND BUT ARE PROBABLY THE BEST THINGS EVER IN THE FISHTORY OF THE SEAVERSE!!!

It all looks so cool.

"Mom!" I say, stabbing my fin so hard into the newspaper it goes right through and plonks Dad on the hammer. "Can I have one of these? Please, please? Pretty please with a side order of please?"

Dad looks at me angrily through the hole in the paper, and Mom catches

285

the two crab tarts as they pop out of the toaster. "No!" they both say at exactly the same time, like they've been practicing.

"Why?" I ask, cutting around the ad with my fin so that I can stick it on my wall.

"Because it's bad for you," Mom says, finally bringing my breakfast over.

BAD FOR ME?!

I stare at her so hard my eyes nearly pop out of my hammer. What is wrong with her? How can something so good be bad?!

"You should be out playing with your friends, not stuck at home playing a silly

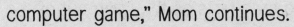

computer game," Mom continues.

SILLY?! I'm starting to think Mom might actually have gone crazy.

"But, Mom, I'd have way more friends to play with if I had one of these. I'd be the most popular shark in Shark Point!"

But Mom just shakes her head. "There's no way I'm changing my mind, Harry. Anyway, you should be concentrating on your studying at the moment."

I can't believe she's being so mean! I'm her son. Her only son. Doesn't my happiness mean anything to her?

"I have rights, you know!" I say, puffing up my chest and sticking out my dorsal fin.

Mom looks at me like I've just broken her best vase with a finball.

"I do! I'll list them for you if you don't believe me."

Mom stares at me. "Go on, then."

"Oh, well, uh, number one: I have the right to—uh—to develop proper fin—eye coordination!"

Mom just rolls her eyes.

"Number two: I—uh—uh—I have the right to express myself through getting the highest score at Super Snapper Races 8!"

Mom starts tapping her fin on the counter.

"Number three: I have the right to new technology. I should not be left behind in the backwater of old stuff where all you old sharks live!" (I think I might be going too far, but I can't seem to stop now . . .)

TAP
TAP
TAP

"Number four: I have the right to have parents who love

me enough to give me what I need to become a happy and healthy hammer-head shark!"

The kitchen is silent, except for a few pops and crackles as the last of my kelp krispies finally turn to mush. Mom is glaring so hard at me I turn to Dad.

"Tell her, Dad—I need a Fintendo, don't I?"

Dad peers over the top of the paper, but he isn't looking at me, he's looking at Mom. "Harry, you definitely need some-thing . . . ," he says.

Yayyyyyyyyyyyyy!

"You need to be grounded for a week and get no fin money for a month if you don't apologize for upsetting your mom, right now!"

Oh.

Mom looks really angry. She snatches the ad from my fin, crumples it up, and throws it into the trash can.

"Now, you listen to me, Harry," she says. "If you don't start studying and pass your exams, not only will you *not* be getting a Fintendo, but you won't be going to the end-of-year party either!"

Mom takes my breakfast (I hadn't even

started eating it!) and throws the bowl in the dishwasher. Then she crosses her fins and stares at me.

I don't believe it. No Fintendo. No breakfast. And the threat of no end-of-school party!

THIS IS SO UNFAIR.

I bang my hammer on the table. "I can't believe how mean you're being. You're lucky I don't report you to the National Society for the Prevention of Cruelty to Hammerheads!"

With that, I storm out of the kitchen and swim to my bedroom as fast as my tail will propel me.

I throw myself onto my bed and pound the seaweed blanket with my fins.

"What's up, Harry?" Humphrey, my humming-fish alarm clock, says. Lenny the lantern fish (my bedside lamp) lights up and shines his glow on me.

"I am never, ever, ever, as long as I live, getting out of bed again," I wail, burrowing under the covers. "I am now the prisoner of the most evil dictator in the fishtory of shark-kind."

"Who's that?" asks Lenny.

"MY MOM!!!!!!!!!" I shout from under the covers. "She doesn't care about my happiness. All she wants me to do

is study, study, study—and she knows how much I hate studying. She is so evil she makes the sting of sting-rays feel like tickles, and the chomp of a great white feel like a kiss from your granny!"

"I think I'd rather be chomped by a great white," says Humphrey. "My granny smells like boiled sea cabbage and has lips like a sea cow's rear end."

"Whatever!" I whine, sticking an eye out from under the cover. "My mom's evil, evil Mrs. McEvil from Evilville-on-Sea!"

Just then Mom swims into the room, carrying my lunch box and a tray. The tray contains a bowl of fresh kelp krispies and a plate of crab Pop-Tarts.

"I'm sorry I shouted at you, Harry, but you did make me very angry," Mom says. "Now make sure you have a big breakfast. You want to have plenty of energy for your schoolwork." She puts the tray down beside my bed and tucks my lunch box into my backpack. "I've put an extra bag of krilled chips in your

295

lunch box so you don't go hungry during the day."

"Wow," Humphrey says as Mom swims out of the room. "That sounds like the most evil breakfast and lunch box ever. What an evil dictator your mom is!"

Humphrey and Lenny start to snicker behind their fins.

"It's just an act!" I shout. "She *is* evil! You didn't hear what she said to me in the kitchen." But Humphrey and Lenny

are now floating on their backs, surrounded by giggle bubbles.

"Hey, Harry," says a voice at the window. I look up and see my best friends—Ralph the pilot fish, Joe the jellyfish, and Tony the tiger shark—crowded at the windowsill. "Want a game of finball before school?" Ralph says with a grin. Tony heads a ball toward Joe, who clutches it in twelve of his legs, then uses a massive toot to aim it at my bedroom window. I dive out of bed and flick it away with my tail.

Saved!

I grab my backpack and a finful of

crab Pop-Tarts and head for the window.

"I thought you were never getting out of bed again!" Humphrey calls after me. He and Lenny start laughing their heads off again as I swim away.

By the time I get to the park, I've calmed down a bit, but then we hear a crowd approaching.

"Wow!"

"WOW!!"

"WOW WOW WOW!!!"

"WOW!!! WOW!!! WOW!!! WOW!!!"

A stream of our class friends come

through the park gates, flapping their fins in excitement.

"What's going on?" Tony says, swimming above us to get a better look. I push up to join him. They're all crowded around the broad back of a young bull shark.

"It's Billy," says Ralph, swimming up with Joe. "What's he holding?"

The other kids are all looking at something Billy has in his fins. I turn on my hammer-vision and use it to zoom in on the center of the crowd.

My stomach flips.

Billy is holding a new Fintendo SeaWii-DS!

He's playing Super Snapper Races 8
like a pro. His fins are flying across the
controls and his eyes are fixed on the
screen. I click off my hammer-vision and
kick down toward him. I have to get a
closer look at the console. Billy must
have the best parents ever if they've

bought him a Fintendo on the day it comes out!

Ralph and the others follow me as I shoulder my way through the crowd.

When I finally catch a glimpse of it, I can't believe my eyes. It's as shiny as a black sea crystal and buzzing with noise and color. It looks even better in real life than it does in the ad. Billy finishes the level he's on and hits a new high score.

The crowd goes wild!

I push up to him. "Billy, your Fintendo's awesome! Can I try?"

Billy looks up from the console and

glares at me. "No way! I'm not lending this to anyone." He swims off toward the park gates.

The crowd moves on, following Billy like he's the coolest thing in the whole ocean.

It's so unfair! How come Billy gets a Fintendo and I don't? It's official—I have the evilest mom in the ocean!

CHAPTER 2

I don't feel any better by the time school starts, and my mood is not helped by our sea-turtle teacher, Mrs. Shelby. She keeps droning on and on about studying for our exams. It's like being at home with Mom!

How do they expect me to think about exams now that I've actually seen a new

Fintendo? I stare out of the window at the girls playing flounder ball. I'm not really that interested, but it's certainly more interesting than Mrs. Shelby's fish-tory review.

"*Harry!*"

I jump as Mrs. Shelby yells at me.

"Yes, Mrs. Shelby?"

"Do you think you can tell me about King Moby the Eighth's first wife, Harry?"

"His first wife was called Harry?" I say without thinking. My cheeks start to turn red as I realize the silly mistake I've made.

"No, Harry," Mrs. Shelby continues, looking irritated. "Can you tell me her actual name?"

Ralph, who's at the desk next to me, whispers the answer into my ear. I turn back to Mrs. Shelby. "His first wife was called Catherine of Plankton."

Mrs. Shelby narrows her sea-turtle eyes. "Correct. And what happened to her?"

I sneak a look at Ralph, who shrugs. I look across the room and see Joe, who pretends to scratch his head with some of his tentacles so Mrs. Shelby can't see his face.

"I don't know," Joe mouths unhelpfully. Great!

I can hear Rick Reef and his sidekick Donny Dogfish snickering at me from the back of the room. My hammer is turning pinker than a prawnburger.

Mrs. Shelby sighs and points back at the interactive whitebait-board. "For the benefit of Harry—and anyone else who wasn't listening—Moby the Eighth was King of Fingland from 1509 to 1547. He had six wives—Catherine of Plankton, whom he divorced; Anne Boatlyn, whom he had beheaded; Jane Seamour, who died giving birth to Moby's only son, Seaweed—who lived until he was just sixteen."

I bet King Moby wouldn't have put up with not having a Fintendo. He always seemed to get what he wanted.

"Then came Anne of Waves," Mrs. Shelby continues, "whom Moby divorced because he didn't like how she looked.

After Anne, Moby married Catherine Sea-Coward, who hated Moby so much that she had lots of other boyfriends—so Moby had her beheaded too."

Moby is sounding pretty evil by now—not as evil as my mom, but getting there.

"Last, Moby married Catherine Starfish.

Unfortunately, they also had no children, but stayed married until Moby died in 1547, leaving his only living child, Elobsterbeth, to become Queen."

I look around the class. It turns out that everyone else, even Rick and Donny, have been writing all this down. I haven't written

a word. I've been too busy being annoyed at Mom and comparing her to Moby the Eighth. I lean over to Ralph to ask him if I can copy his notes later—but before I can say a word, the bell rings for recess.

"Wait, please!" Mrs. Shelby shouts as everyone starts getting up from their desks. "Before you go, I have an important announcement to make about the end-of-year party."

Everyone stops dead and listens. The end-of-year party is the best thing about school. Which makes Mom double-evil for threatening to not let me go. Mrs. Shelby pushes her little round glasses up her flat turtle face. "In fact, I have some very exciting news about the party."

We all stare at her, wide-eyed and openmouthed. What could it be?

"This year," Mrs. Shelby announces grandly, "there will be a competition to find the best dancer in the whole school!"

Is that it? I thought she said it was going to be EXCITING news. There's nothing exciting about dancing. All the boys start to groan. But the dolphin twins, Pearl and Cora, start

swimming around with glee, high-finning and whooping. I don't know why they're so happy. Dancing is dorky, and I can make a list to prove it. Dancing is stupid because:

1. Anyone doing it looks like they're desperate to go to the bathroom.

2. The only kids interested in dancing are girls, and who wants to look like a girl?!

3. The only other underwater creatures who enjoy dancing are SEA SPONGES who have nothing better to do on a Saturday night than watch *Dancing with the Starfish*.

4. Seriously. Isn't that enough to put anyone off dancing FOR LIFE???

While I've been making my ultra-important list, Mrs. Shelby has been making one of her own—listing all the reasons why dancing is great! Things like it's really good exercise, it's a great way of making friends, and it's so much fun. I can hardly believe my ears. Is she crazy?!

"And finally," Mrs. Shelby says, her voice all squeaky with excitement, "whoever comes in first in the end-of-year dance contest will win a special prize!"

Hmmm, I wonder what that will be? A pink sparkly leotard and glittery fin warmers?

"The dancer with the best routine,"

Mrs. Shelby says, "will win a brand-new Fintendo SeaWii-DS!"

OMC! (Oh. My. Cod.)

I'm so shocked, my hammer head actually hits the desk. Mrs. Shelby looks at me all worried.

I pick my face up and try to make my mouth speak, but it's not easy. "W . . . wh . . . what did you say, Mrs. Shelby?"

Mrs. Shelby shakes her head. "Oh, Harry, I'm going to have to have a word with your parents. You haven't listened to a word I've said all this time!"

"No—no—NO, Mrs. Shelby. I was listening . . . I'm just not sure I heard that

314

last part right. Could you say it again?"

Mrs. Shelby gives a big sigh. "I said that the student who does the best dance routine of the contest will win a brand-new Fintendo SeaWii-DS."

"That's what I thought," I say, and then everything becomes a big blur. All I can think about is the prize.

"Are you all right, Harry?" Tony says as we swim out to the playground.

An actual Fintendo!

"Open your mouth,

Harry, I need a break-time snack," Ralph says.

A brand new Fintendo—for free!

I look around. Pearl and Cora have already taken over a corner of the playground and are busy practicing their ballet moves.

"You sure you're all right, pal?" Ralph asks.

I nod. "Never better! Want to know why?"

Ralph's eyes widen hopefully. "Because you're going to let me snack on your leftover crab Pop-Tarts?"

I shake my head. "No. Because I'm

going to win a Fintendo and it's going to be the easiest thing EVER!"

"You're going to dance?" Ralph laughs as I start flexing my fins and limbering up my hammer.

"You've always said dancing was dumb," says Joe. Purple flashes of confusion start running up and down his tentacles.

"Dancing *is* dumb," I say with a smile. "And that's exactly why I'm going to win!"

Joe's whole body starts flashing purple. "But . . . "

FLUBBBBBBERRRRRRRRR!!!!

Suddenly my head is shaking and the

world looks like it's made of quivering rubber.

I hear Rick snickering behind me. He's sneaked up and *boinged* my hammer. Ralph and Joe catch hold of each end of my head to try to stop it from flubbering.

"You? Dance?" Rick sneers. "You couldn't dance your way out of a dead clam!"

"I-I-I . . . can . . . d-d-d-dance!" I stammer. My voice is all over the place—I sound like a Super Mario Carp backfiring on the starting grid.

As my flubbering head slows down,

Rick's pointy face comes into focus. He leans right into my hammer, his nose stuck between my eyes.

"That Fintendo is mine, Harry, and no goofy little stammerhead is going to get in my way!"

CHAPTER 3

I spend the rest of the day hardly able to concentrate on anything. When the final bell rings I zoom out of school, leaving Ralph and the others behind in a cloud of *WHOOSH!!!* I don't think I've ever gotten home so quickly.

I hardly notice the delicious smell of

freshly baked fish cakes coming from the kitchen. I fly up the stairs and hook my tail on the top banister to swing me around the coral corridor at insane speed.

"Harry, is that you? Do you want a fish c—?" is all I hear from Mom before I slam the door behind me, head for my desktop P-Sea, and flick it on.

I need to surf the interwet, and I need to surf the interwet NOW.

Humphrey and Lenny float toward me and start looking over my shoulder.

"You still sulking, Harry?" Humphrey asks as the P-Sea boots up.

"Oh no! What's that smell?" Lenny says, stifling a giggle. "Could it be your evil dictator mom making some deadly fish cakes? Shall we inform the authorities?"

"No, thank you," I tell them calmly.

The screen flickers to life. I do a quick search for the site I need. . . .

"'The Life and Times of Moby the Eighth'?" Lenny reads. "Harry, what are you doing?"

"Studying, of course," I tell them.

"But you hate studying!" Lenny exclaims, his light blinking.

"Not anymore," I say.

"But . . . ," says Humphrey.

"I don't understand . . . ," says Lenny.

I sigh and turn to look at them. "If I don't study, I won't pass my exams, and if I don't pass my exams, I can't go to the end-of-year party, and if I can't go to the end-of-year party, I won't be able to enter the dance competition, and if I can't enter the dance competition—"

"You won't turn into a girl?" says Humphrey.

"No," I say. "If I can't enter the dance competition, then I can't win the dance competition, and if I can't win the dance competition, I can't swim

away with a new Fintendo SeaWii-DS. And I REALLY want a new Fintendo SeaWii-DS. Now can you please be quiet? I have a ton of catching up to do!"

I turn back to the screen and start to read.

I wake up the next morning with my head on the P-Sea's keyboard and my chin covered in sleepy drool.

I must have fallen asleep studying.

I stretch my aching body and head downstairs. It's Saturday, so I'll have plenty of time to study once I'm feeling a bit more awake. Dad comes swimming out of the kitchen with a finful of shrimp Pop-Tarts. I grab a couple for breakfast and look at Dad with my best hopeful goggly eyes.

Dad sighs and digs into his pocket.

He brings out but-
tons, an old, rusty
key, some coral
marbles, and (finally!)
his wallet.

Saturday is fin money day, and I
always spend it on a copy of *Ready,
Steady, SHARK!*—my favorite sports
magazine. This week I can't wait to get
it, because they've got an interview
with the world-famous underwater
sharklete Turbo Tex.

"Are you all right, Harry?" Dad
says as he hands me my money. "You
look really tired."

"Oh, I was just up late studying," I say casually.

Dad's eyes widen in surprise. "Really?"

I nod.

"Well, that's very good to hear. Very good indeed." He slaps me on the back. "Keep at it and one day you might even be as clever as me!"

"That would be cool, Dad!" I say with a grin.

After quickly eating my Pop-Tarts I head out to Shark Point. The water is still cool, but I hardly notice. One half of my mind is on Turbo Tex, and the other is on the Fintendo I'm going to win at the end of the year. Then, suddenly, I hear a girl's voice.

"No, you should do a tail-twist with an overkick."

I look around and see Pearl and Cora on the opposite side of the street. They've got their bags over their shoulders and they're wearing sparkly pink fin warmers. They're so deep in conversation they don't even notice me.

"Then I'll do a plié, followed by a pirouette," Cora says.

A WHAT followed by a WHAT?

"Ooh, yes," says Pearl. "That would

be perfect! We are so going to win this dance competition!"

The girls high-fin and keep going down the street. So they were talking about dancing. Hmmm. This gives me an idea. Maybe they're going off to practice somewhere. I could spy on them and see if I can get a few tips for my own routine.

I drift over to the shadows at the edge of the street and start following them. I don't need to worry about being seen, though—they're way too busy talking about their own moves.

I follow the twins all the way to a

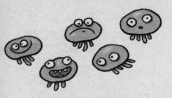

building on the outskirts of town. They swim up some rickety old stairs and disappear inside. I hear the faint sound of a piano playing. I've come too far to turn back now—if I'm going to learn a few dance moves from the girls, I'm going to have to look inside.

I creep up the stairs. As I reach the door at the top, the music gets louder, and I can hear the swishing of several tails. The door isn't completely shut, so I float up close to it and place a goggly eye by the gap. It takes a few seconds for my eye to adjust to the bright lights inside. The wall opposite me is covered with mirror-carp scales. A sign at the top of the wall reads:

MADAME L'OCTOPUS'S BALLET STUDIO

Ballet!

I'm not doing any ballet in my dance routine—that's way too girly.

Pearl and Cora have joined a group of girl fish and dolphins. They're all dressed in pink ballet gear and they're warming up to the music.

There's nothing useful for me here. I start to swim away. But suddenly a thick, rubbery octopus tentacle shoots

through the door and grabs me by the tail!

I'm hauled into the room with a *thud*, and suddenly there's a huge greeny-pink face staring into mine. A high-pitched voice with a Trench accent screams in my ear.

"And what do we 'ave 'ere?"

"Harry!" Pearl yells.

"It's Harry Hammer, Madame L'Octopus," Cora says. "He goes to our school."

Madame L'Octopus stares at me. "And he is a ballet dancer, *oui*?"

"Well, I know he's good at dancing," Pearl says.

I stare at her in shock.

Pearl grins back at me. "Because he's

MADAME L'OCTOPUS'S BALLET STUDIO

been telling everyone he's going to win the school dance competition."

"Veeery interesting," says Madame L'Octopus, waving me around in her huge tentacle. "Eet is about time we had a boy in this class. Let us see what the leetle dancey hammerhead can do."

The girls all giggle and start to clap along with the music. Madame L'Octopus lets go of me, but I can't escape. She's standing right between me and the door.

I'm trapped.

I can feel my face turning pink. I can't let Pearl and Cora see that I know nothing about dancing. They'll tell Rick and I'll be the laughingstock of the school—again!

I think back to what I overheard the twins talking about on the way here. What was it? Pliers? Piro-nets? I have no idea what those moves are, but I have to do something. So I start waving my tail in time to the music and nodding my hammer backward and forward.

"I do believe 'ee can do ballet!" Madame L'Octopus cries, twirling around in a cloud of ink and rippling her tentacles with joy.

Hmmm, maybe this isn't going to be

so difficult after all. Feeling a bit braver, I try to speed up. But then . . .

1. The girls form a circle around me, beating their fins in time.

2. I attempt a piro-net on my tail end (even though I don't actually know what that is) and clatter into a young hermit crab.

3. The hermit crab spins into Madame L'Octopus's mouth and causes her to have a coughing fit.

4. The coughing fit makes Madame L'Octopus squirt out a huge cloud of ink.

5. And suddenly no one can see where they are or where they're going.

6. And I crash into about ten girls.

7. And I end up with my hammer covered in mirror-carp scales, a pink fin warmer on my dorsal, and someone's frilly ballet skirt on my head!

As the ink clears, Cora and Pearl swim right up in front of me with their SeaBerry

smartphones—and start taking pictures!

"Oh my cod! Everyone's gonna love this on Plaicebook!" Pearl shrieks.

Disaster!

"*You!*" Madame L'Octopus shrieks, pointing all of her eight tentacles at me. "*You!!!*"

"Me, what?" I say, pulling the skirt off my head.

"You have ruined my mirror!"

We all turn to look at the far wall. The mirror-carp scales have all gone. Everyone looks back at me. The mirror-carp scales are now covering my skin. Some of the girls start checking their reflection in me! As fast as I can, I start flicking the scales off with my tail.

"You have to pay!" Madame L'Octopus yells, wrapping one of her tentacles around me. "You must pay for zee damage!"

"But—but . . . ," I stammer.

"But what?" she hisses.

"But I don't have any money," I reply. "Well, only my fin money . . ."

"Zat will do!" she snaps.

I stare at her.

She glares back.

"Give eet to me, then!"

Pearl and Cora start fiddling with their phones, ready to take another picture of me. I quickly take my fin money out of my pocket and give it to her.

"Now go!" Madame L'Octopus yells.

If she wasn't so scary, I'd yell back, "Don't worry, I'm gone!" But she is scary—very scary—so I don't say a word and just swim for the door.

As soon as I get outside, I bang my hammer against the wall in despair. It's so unfair! I didn't even want to go to a dorky ballet class. I only came out to get a copy of *Ready, Steady, SHARK!*—and now I can't afford it!

I am totally fed up and completely broke. I brush the rest of the mirror-carp scales off me and start swimming home.

"Wow! You're so miserable you look like you've been given turtle-toe jam for lunch!" a girl's voice says as I turn the corner.

Brilliant. Another girl who wants to make fun of me.

Could today get any worse?

CHAPTER 4

I spin around, thinking it might be one of the girls from the ballet class. But it isn't.

A young leopard shark swims in front of me. She's wearing a cool Pike tracksuit. Her cap is on back-to-front and her neck is dripping with shipwreck bling.

"So, what's up?" she asks, giving me a fin bump. "Why you lookin' so stressed? I'm Lola, by the way. And you're Harry Hammer, aren't you?"

I look at her, confused. "Yeah—uh—how do you know?"

Lola grins. "Seen you with your dad in the newspapers."

"Oh." I'm not sure if she's about to make fun of me, so I don't smile back.

"It's all right. I don't bite," Lola says. "Just saw you looking all grumpy, so I

thought I'd see what the matter was. You don't have to tell me if you don't want to, though."

Lola's smile looks friendly, so I explain what happened back at the ballet school, and about the competition and the Fintendo prize.

Lola snorts with laughter, but it's not mean like Rick's—it's much more sympathetic.

"So you want to learn to dance?"

I nod.

"Well, you're not going to learn how to win the competition at ballet school. Ballet's really boring, isn't it?"

344

"I suppose."

"Real dancing's learned on the street."

I frown. "What do you mean?"

Lola starts spinning on the spot before doing a backflip and a star-fin. "See?" she says with a smile. "Want me to show you how?"

Suddenly I feel a million times better. "Yes, please!"

Lola nods. "Let's go to the skate park. I'll have you break-dancing in no time!"

"Oh . . . I . . . I can't go there."

Lola puts her fins on her hips and frowns at me. "Why not?"

"Well—uh—my mom says I'm not

allowed over there." I feel my face start to burn.

Lola shakes her head. "Are you some kind of mama's shark? Maybe I should just take you back to ballet class, then!"

"No!" I yell. "I want to learn how to break-dance and I don't care where I have to go to do it. I've got to win that Fintendo!"

Lola zooms past me, barrel-rolling into a skimming rush right past my hammer. Then she flicks out her fins and finishes with her tail bent up and her fins thrown back. It's the most brilliant dance move I've ever seen. "You sure

346

you want to dance like this, Harry? It's not for mama's sharks, you know!"

Right now I want nothing more than for Lola to show me how to dance. She is one of the coolest sharks I have EVER met!

I nod again, this time totally sure.

"Come on, then!"

And *BANG!* She's off like a rocket.

We shoot down narrow alleys and through dark, dingy streets, heading toward South Central Shark Point. I've never been to this part of Shark Point before. The walls are covered in graffiti and there are no houses, just coral buildings and chain-link fences. We head past a load of closed-down shops and a row of empty factories. The fish and sharks around us seem bigger and scarier than the ones I'm used to. I can hear police sirens not too far away, and whale trains thunder

overhead, dragging cargoes of ship-wreck metal.

Eventually we come to the skate park. Behind rusty fences, the park is alive with sharks of all shapes and sizes. All of them are wearing Pike or FishHead sports gear. A gang of leopard sharks are riding yellow-finned skateboards.

"All right, Leon!" Lola calls to the nearest leopard shark. He looks around and jumps off his skateboard. Then he waves a fin to the others, and one by one the group coasts to a halt, looking at me suspiciously.

Lola looks back at me. "Harry, this is

my dance crew—the Shark Beatz." Lola turns back to the gang. "Don't worry, boys, this is Harry. He's cool."

The Shark Beatz don't seem so sure, though. Leon flicks his tail over and stares at me with narrow eyes. "He doesn't look that cool to me."

"I told you, he's all right." Lola turns to me. "This is Leon.

He's my brother, and he's not as mean as he thinks he is."

Leon frowns, but doesn't say anything. He doesn't stop staring at me, though.

Lola beckons me forward with her fin. "Harry wants to learn how to dance. I brought him here so we could show him how to bust some moves."

The Shark Beatz start to laugh out loud. Leon cracks a huge smile. "A hammerhead? Dance? Do me a favor. All hammerheads are good for is knocking ships' nails into timber."

Lola nudges Leon. "Clam it. He needs our help, and we're going to give it to him, okay?"

I look at Lola. I'm not used to someone sticking up for me like this. It's making me feel a bit funny. I really hope it's not showing on my face. I stretch up to my full height. "Lola says you guys are the best dancers in all of Shark Point."

They nod.

"Well, I want to learn from the best."

This seems to do the trick, as the group all put their skateboards aside and form a circle around us.

Leon takes his phone from his pocket and starts playing a really cool ship-hop tune.

Lola starts flicking her tail back and forth to the beat. "Let's start with the most basic move—the Six Tail."

Lola and Leon go down on their bent tails, flicking them around in a circle and balancing their bodies on their fins behind them. They do six complete circles, then stop and stare at me.

"Go, Hammer!" Leon calls.

I start to bend my tail, trip over it, and smash my hammer in the worst self-*FLUBBERRRRRRRRRRR* of all time.

Great.

My boinging head flubbers back and forth, and when it finally stops, Leon and the rest of the Shark Beatz are floating on their backs, holding their stomachs, laughing. I try the Six Tail again. This time I bend, circle, fin-balance, and *CRASH*.

Lola offers me a fin. "This might take longer

FLUBBBBERRRR

than I thought," she says kindly as she pulls me back up.

Over the next couple of hours, the Shark Beatz show me how to do all of their best moves:

1. The Catfish Daddy (all loose fins and wobbly head).

2. The Treasure-Chest Pop (waves through the chest and a dorsal slap).

3. The Plop, Rock, and Drop (a combination of a tail-plop, a body-rock, and falling over—I do the falling over part REALLY well. I'm just terrible at catching myself on my fins).

4. The Hammer-Dock (they made that one up especially for me). And then it's time for the hardest move of all . . .
5. The Head-Spin!

Lola turns herself upside down and, with a flick of her fins, starts to rotate on her head. She gets faster and faster as Leon and the Shark Beatz cheer her on. She whirs and blurs until I can't see her because she's moving so fast. Then *BANG!* She storms to a stop, fins out, tail flicked up to her dorsal, hanging there like the most rad thing of all time.

We all start cheering. But almost immediately I feel gloomy.

How can I ever do anything as good as that?

"Your turn, Hammer!" Lola calls as all of the Shark Beatz swim up to her, finning her on the back.

"Okay!" I shout, and flip myself upside down.

I flick out with my fins. Because of my big, flubbery hammer, it takes a lot more work to get myself moving than it does a sleek and beautiful leopard shark like Lola, but eventually I start to spin.

The whole world starts to revolve as I flick and kick.

Kick and flick.

As I get faster, it's easier and easier to move through the water. The skate park becomes spinning streaks of color . . .

I'm doing it.

I'm doing the hardest ship-hop move of all time.

The Head-Spin!

I'm amazing!

I'm awesome!

I'm a DANCER!

I'M A DANCER!!!

Even the Shark Beatz are cheering me

on. They're cheering and cheering and . . .

And . . . actually . . . it doesn't sound that much like cheering . . .

It sounds more like . . .

SCREAMING.

BOOOOOOOSH! I crash out of the Head-Spin and bounce onto the coral floor with a painful crunch.

I look up dizzily.

Everyone is spinning around me as if I'm still in the Head-Spin. But I can feel the rough coral against my back. It's NOT ME who's spinning.

IT'S THEM!

Then I realize what's happened . . .

My ridiculous hammer is so big, I've created an enormous whirlpool in the middle of the skate park!

Everyone is tumbling head over tail around me like socks in a washing machine. NOOOOOOOOOOOOOOOOOOO!!!!!!!

Okay, I've messed up big-time.

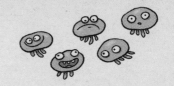

I'm in a new place, throwing a group of tough sharks around like tadpoles in a sea tornado, and they are all screaming their heads off.

I am going to be in trouble so big, a word has yet to be invented for how GIGANTI-HUGE it's going to be. I cover my hammer with my fins and wait for the Shark Beatz to swim down and teach me a very painful lesson.

Except something I'm not expecting to happen happens. . . .

1. The screaming in the whirlpool starts to change.

2. The screams of fear become high-pitched screams of laughter.
3. As the whirlpool caused by my hammer starts to slow down, there's even more laughter.
4. I uncover my eyes and see the Shark Beatz holding on to one another and laughing.
5. And as they all slow down and gain control of their fins and tails, they start cheering!
6. Cheering ME!!!!

"Ham-MER! Ham-MER!! HAM-MERRRR-RRRRRRRR!!!!" they chant together. Leon has the widest smile on his face, and Lola swims down and hugs me tight in her fins! This makes me go all goggly-eyed.

362

"Wow, Harry, that was amazing!" Lola says. "That was the greatest Head-Spin we have ever seen. None of us have ever caused a whirlpool before!"

We all grab fins, touch tails, and dance around like clown fish in a carnival—madly whooping, high-finning, and generally laughing the teeth right out of our gums!

Even Leon comes over and shakes me by the fin. "Dude, I'm sorry I ever doubted you. You are going to be a totally radical dancer. You're FINtastic!"

And I *feel* FINtastic!

CHAPTER 5

It's the first day of the exams and we're all waiting for Mrs. Shelby to hand out our papers. At his desk across the room, Joe is turning a frightened shade of yellow. At the desk next to me, Ralph is trying to remember what happened to each of Moby the Eighth's wives.

"Divorced, beheaded, divorced—no, died," he mutters. "Divorced—or was that one beheaded?" He looks at Tony. Tony is staring into space and flicking his tail nervously. Even Rick looks uneasy

as he chews on his pencil fish. But for the first time ever, I don't feel too bad about having to take an exam. Over the past few weeks I've spent more time studying than

I've spent eating kelp krispies—and that's a lot! And when I haven't been studying, or eating kelp krispies, I've been learning how to dance at the skate park with Lola. Now I feel ready to take on anything!

"Make sure you take your time with your answers," Mrs. Shelby says as she starts handing out the exams. "You don't want to make any silly mistakes."

I look down at the first question.

EXAM

What was King Moby's favorite sport?

a) Finball ☐
b) Flounder ball ☐
c) Hunting ☐

Hunting! I know because it came up when I was doing some last-minute reviewing this morning on my P-Sea.

I quickly check the answer. Then I read the next question.

What was the name of
King Moby's daughter?
a) Seaweedia ☐
b) Elobsterbeth ☐
c) Crabella ☐

Yes! I know that one too—I learned it when I got Humphrey and Lenny

to pretend to be Moby's children the other day. It was partly to help me with my reviewing and partly to get back at them for teasing me about Mom not being evil.

I carefully check the Elobsterbeth box with my pencil fish. Then I go on to the next question.

What did King Moby
wear on his head?
   a) A starfish   ☐
   b) A jellyfish   ☐
   c) A crown fish   ☐

Crown fish! And so it goes. Before I know it, I've finished the final question. I look around the classroom. The others are all still writing. I stare out the window and start going through my dance routine in my head. Thanks to Lola's teaching, my Catfish Daddy is going really well. I start wobbling my head and waving my fins as I imagine myself at the dance contest. The other contestants are all cheering, the judges are clapping their fins in time, and I'm—

"Harry! What are you doing?"

I jump in shock. Mrs. Shelby is floating next to my desk, glaring at me.

"Why are you wobbling your head? Why aren't you doing your exam?" she snaps.

"I've finished, Mrs. Shelby."

Mrs. Shelby sighs and shakes her head. "I told you not to rush, Harry. Rushing causes mistakes." She looks down at my paper. "Oh." She starts to smile as she reads through my answers. "Okay, well, just sit there quietly until the others have finished. No more head wobbling."

Head wobbling? Doesn't Mrs. Shelby know a Catfish Daddy when she sees one?! But I can't help grinning. Who'd have thought that studying would make exams almost fun?

The week of the exams goes by faster than a rocket fish. I get a bit muddled up in Trench and get some of my answers wrong in math, but mostly things go way better than normal. And the best thing is, Mom's so pleased with the way I studied that she's said I can go to the end-of-school party no matter what I get.

The day before the party, I go to the skate park for one last practice. Lola and Leon are there waiting for me. Lola's

holding something for me in her fin.

"I got you this," she says, looking a bit embarrassed. "It's to bring you good luck at the dance contest."

She swims closer to me. She's holding a thick anchor chain decorated in shipwreck bling. It's almost as big as Leon's.

"Cool! Thanks," I say as she goes to put it on me. Luckily, it's big enough to fit over my hammer head.

"And I got you something too," Leon says with a grin. He hands me a baseball cap. It's got SHARK BEATZ studded in coral on the front.

"Wow!"

"Now you're really one of the crew," Lola says, grinning.

"What, really?" I say, my eyes goggling in shock.

"Yeah, bro," Leon says with a high fin. "You're our number one Head-Spinner."

"And you're going to win that dance contest for sure!" Lola

does a quick backflip. "Come on, let's go and practice some Hammer-Docks."

Lola and Leon head off to the middle of the park. As I swim after them, I feel like the happiest hammerhead alive. I've finished my exams and I'm allowed to go to the party. Now all I have to do is win the Fintendo!

And, for once in my life, I feel absolutely certain that nothing—and I mean NOTHING—can possibly go wrong.

CHAPTER 6

OH MY COD!

I've passed every exam I took with flying colors! Mrs. Shelby pats me on the head as I reread the results just to make sure. But it's true—I've come in first in almost everything! I am thirty-three tail flips and a shark smile happy!

Mom and Dad are just as excited when I get home from school and tell them the good news. We swim happy circles around the kitchen and knock a box of kelp krispies over. The krispies float through the water and start sticking to our skin. All three of us look like we've been covered in barnacles!

Then Dad shakes my fin. "Well done, son," he says, wiping a kelp krispie from his eye. "We're so proud of you."

"Yes we are!" says Mom, giving me a massive hug. "Well done, starfish! Now you can really enjoy the end-of-year party tonight."

I get a sudden fluttery feeling in my tummy.

Now that I've passed my exams, it's time for me to bag that Fintendo!

The school gym has been decorated for the end-of-year party. Well, when I say "decorated," what I mean is that a few strings of Christmas lights have been strung up and a huge glitter-pearl is hanging from the ceiling. A couple of really bored-looking lantern fish are taking turns to shine on it.

"I don't think much of the music," Joe mutters.

Ralph and Tony nod in agreement.

The DJ (also known as Mrs. Shelby) is playing some awful music from the olden days. They're songs my mom and dad like!

A table of snacks is set up against the far wall. Two rows of chairs line the

long walls on either side of the hall. One side has the boys sitting on them, the other has the girls. Each line is staring at the other, but not saying a word.

Pearl and Cora are in their ballet skirts and doing some dance moves. They must be warming up for the contest.

"Are you sure you're going to be able to beat them?" Ralph whispers.

I nod and grin. I haven't told my friends about my street-dancing lessons down at the skate park. I want it to be a surprise.

Then I see Rick and Donny over by the food table. They're tapping their fins to the music. Rick is all dressed up for the contest in his leather jacket and sunglasses. Well, he might look cool now, but seeing me dance will wipe that smirk off his face.

"Oh my cod! Look at that!" Ralph says, pointing a fin toward the dance floor.

Two ancient teachers—Mr. Kelp and Mrs. Clambury—are dancing together. Well, they're trying to dance together, but Mr. Kelp slips, pulls a fin, and has to be helped back to his chair.

It's all majorly embarrassing.

But I'm not really bothered. I'm here for one thing only, and that's the dance contest. I look at the clock, and my tummy churns with nerves. I turn around to chat with Ralph, Joe, and Tony, but they've swum over to the snack table.

I'm just about to join them when Mrs. Shelby stops the music and speaks into the microphone. "Okay, everyone, it's time for the dance contest."

Pearl and Cora start squealing.

"The first round is a dance-off," Mrs. Shelby continues. "Will all contestants please swim over to the dance floor. I want you to all start dancing, and if I call your name, it means you're out. I'll keep going until only three acts are left! There are no rules about what kind of dancing you do. This is your chance to freestyle!"

The music begins and I start going through the moves Lola and the Shark Beatz have been teaching me over the last few weeks. I don't want to get a big hammer or anything, but I can tell that everyone's kind of impressed.

"Where'd you learn to dance like that, Harry?" someone shouts.

"Awesome moves, Harry!" Tony calls. Joe waves his tentacles in time and starts glowing pink with excitement.

"Yeah, yeah, very cool," says Ralph, "but can you please hurry up so I can have something to eat!"

"Billy Bullshark, you're out!" Mrs. Shelby calls through the microphone. "And Sarah Shellfish, I'm afraid you're not going to the next round."

I don't look at anyone else, I just keep focusing on my moves.

"Kevin Killerwhale, I'm afraid you're out too," Mrs. Shelby calls. "Kevin, put your teeth away this minute! And come and see me after the competition. There's no need to be such a bad loser! Lacy Lungfish, nice try, but I'm sorry, you're out."

And so it goes.

I keep on dancing—and hoping with every fin on my body that I won't hear

Mrs. Shelby call my name. And then, suddenly, the music goes silent. I keep on dancing, too scared to stop.

"Harry Hammer!" Mrs. Shelby calls, and my heart sinks.

I'm out!

"Oh, man!" I sigh, swimming over to Ralph, Joe, and Tony. I don't know why they're grinning. Some friends they are!

"Don't look so gloomy, Harry," Mrs. Shelby says. "You've made it to the final."

WHHHHAAAAAAAATTTTTTT?!

I turn around. Only the twins and Rick are left on the dance floor. Ralph, Joe, and Tony start finning and tentacle-ing me on the back. I've done it! I've made it to the next round. It's me against Rick and Pearl and Cora!

"Congratulations, dancers!" Mrs. Shelby cries. "Now it's time for our finalists to perform their individual routines. Pearl and Cora, you're first."

Pearl and Cora fluff up their skirts and start to dance. Although their routine is ballet, it's actually quite good. They twirl and kick and turn in perfect time to the music. As they finish, the crowd goes wild. The twins curtsy and wave as they swim off the dance floor.

"Next up, Rick Reef!" Mrs. Shelby cries.

Rick swims to the center of the dance floor and starts doing the coolest dive-jive I have ever seen. The light bouncing off the glitter-pearl sparkles on his blue-whale shoes and his tail is a blur.

Rick finishes with a fin-stand and an awesome dorsal flip.

It's so good, even I'm clapping!

Then, suddenly, I

feel scared. If I'm not even cooler than Rick and even more graceful than the dolphin twins, that Fintendo is never going to be mine.

I take my Shark Beatz cap and shipwreck bling out of my pocket and put them on. I'm going to have to pull out all the stops.

And that means I'm going to have to do my signature move—the immense Hammerhead Head-Spin!

The music booms out. I start busting every move that Lola and the Shark Beatz have drilled into me.

"Go, Harry!" Ralph yells.

"Come on!" Joe and Tony shout, clapping their tentacles and fins in time.

I am a ship-hop king! Just like Moby the Eighth (but better at dancing and without all the headless wives). The light from the glitter-pearl starts bouncing off my bling and reflecting all around the room. I start Six-Tailing in circles across the floor. My cap is on backward and my tracksuit is flapping. The music gets faster. I'm Plopping. I'm Docking. I Drop better than I ever have before. The crowd is clapping along. Whooping and yelling.

I am ON FIRE.

One last Treasure-Chest Pop into the

389

coolest Catfish Daddy and I'm upside-down and ready! The Head-Spin starts out well and the gym becomes a blur as I spin faster. But then something terrible happens. . . .

1. My hammer twists the water around me like a ship's propeller . . .
2. In the skate park, this only twirled the spectators around with it . . .
3. But in the closed space of the gym . . . IT'S A DISASTER!

4. CRASH! ARRRRRRRRRRRGH! SPLAT!

   SMASH! OOOOOOOOOOHHHHH!

   BOING! FLUBBBERRRRRRRRRRRRRR!!!

   KERRRRRRRRRRRRRRUNCH!!!!!!!!!

By the time the room stops spinning, everyone is covered in food. And the boy fish are twisted up with the girl fish.

Awkward.

Mrs. Shelby's glasses are upside-down and the rest of the teachers are downside-up. Pearl is somehow wearing Rick's leather jacket, and Rick is floating backward trying to get his tail out of her pink skirt.

Joe and Tony are stuck to the ceiling,

clinging to the glitter-pearl for dear life. Ralph is the only one who seems to be okay. He's been flung into the center of a huge cake and is now happily eating his way out of it.

But I'm right in the middle of the devastation—my hammer still vibrating from the worst self-induced flubber of all time.

Mrs. Shelby staggers out from behind the DJ stand. The other teachers start helping everyone untangle themselves from one another, and wipe the food off their faces.

"HARRY!" Mrs. Shelby yells in her sternest voice. "HARRY!"

"Y-y-y-yes, Mrs. Shelby?"

"You are . . . " Mrs. Shelby pauses to

put her glasses back the right way up.

"Y-y-y-y-yes, Mrs. Shelby?"

"You are DISQUALIFIED!"

I hang my hammer in shame.

"Tonight's winners are Pearl and Cora," Mrs. Shelby says.

Rick lets out a loud boo.

"And it is with great pleasure that

I present you with this prize of a Fintendo SeaWii-DS!"

I'm all ready for this to be the worst moment of my life ever. But then I see the Fintendo. It's pink and glittery and TOTALLY GIRLY.

My Head-Spin may have wrecked the gym, but it gave me the luckiest escape in gaming history. Rick would have made my life misery if I'd won THAT!

And anyway, I might not have a Fintendo, but at least I've passed my exams and won't have to do any more cramming for a very long time. I've got the whole summer vacation ahead of me to hang out with my best buddies. And I'll be able to see lots more of

 my new friends Lola and the Shark Beatz. No, things aren't too bad after all!

When I get home, the house is very quiet. Mom and Dad must be out at some boring event or they've already gone to bed.

My bedroom door is open, but it's dark inside. "Lenny, can I have some light, please," I call to my lantern fish as I swim inside. Nothing happens. I hope I don't have to change his bulb again—it's so tricky and I always get covered in lantern-fish snot.

"SURPRISE!!!!!!!!!!!!!!!!!!!!!!!!!!!!!"

I nearly jump out of my skin as the room is flooded with light. Mom and Dad are standing in the middle of the room, with Humphrey and Lenny. All of them have the biggest smiles on their faces.

"We wanted to give you a special surprise, Harry," Mom says. "To say, 'Well done' for passing your exams and working so hard on your studying."

"Yes," says Dad, "we're very impressed with how seriously you've taken your studies."

Mom laughs. "And to

think I was worried that all you wanted to do was play with a Fintendo!"

I put on my most serious face and shake my head.

"So, to say thank-you for all your hard work . . . ," Mom says, pulling a box out from behind her, "we've bought you this!"

When I see what's on the box, I almost faint in shock. It's a Fintendo!

I can't believe it. I open the box, with trembling fins. Instead of a pink, glittery, GIRLY Fintendo, there's a brilliant blue, awesomely shiny Fintendo—complete with lots of games!

AMAZING!!!!!!!!!!!!!!!!!!!!!!!!!!!

I'm so happy I even hug Mom and Dad without feeling embarrassed. After they leave the room, I high-fin Humphrey and Lenny.

"Still think your mom is an evil dictator, Harry?" laughs Humphrey.

But I don't have time to answer.

I'm too busy firing up Super Snapper Races 8!

THE END

HARRY

Species:

hammerhead shark

You'll spot him . . .

using his special

hammer-vision

Favorite thing:

his Gregor the Gnasher

poster

Most likely to say:

"I wish I was a great white."

Most embarrassing moment: when Mom called him

her "little starfish" in front of all his friends

RALPH

Species:

pilot fish

You'll spot him . . .

eating the food from

between

Harry's teeth!

Favorite thing: shrimp Pop-Tarts

Most likely to say: "So, Harry, what's for

breakfast today?"

Most embarrassing moment: eating too much cake

on Joe's birthday. His face was COVERED in pink

plankton icing.

JOE

Species: jellyfish

You'll spot him . . . hiding behind
Ralph and Harry, or behind his
own tentacles

Favorite thing: his cave, since
it's nice and safe

Most likely to say: "If we do
this, we're going to end up as
fish food. . . ."

Most embarrassing moment:
whenever his rear goes *toot*,
which is when he's scared. Which is all the time.

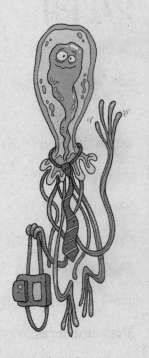

RICK

Species: blacktip reef shark

You'll spot him . . . bullying smaller fish or showing off

Favorite thing: his black leather jacket

Most likely to say: "Last one there's a sea snail!"

Most embarrassing moment: none. Rick's far too cool to get embarrassed.

SHARK BITES

The basking shark is the second-largest fish in existence. Only the whale shark is bigger. Their mouths can be more than three feet in width!

An electric eel does not have teeth. It can grow up to nine feet in length.

Starfish are also known as sea stars. Although most starfish have five arms, some can have as many as twelve!

Piranha are freshwater fish mostly found in the waters of South America. They are carnivorous, which means they eat meat.

Most great white sharks are between thirteen and sixteen feet long and weigh from 1,500 to 2,450 pounds.

The teeth of great white sharks are razor sharp.

SHARK BITES

Sea cows are also known as manatees. They can stay underwater for about fifteen minutes, but must breathe air from the surface in order to survive.

Sharks have been swimming in the world's oceans for over 400 million years.

There are more than four hundred different species of sharks, ranging from the giant hammerhead to the goblin shark.

Sharks do not have bones. They are cartilaginous fish, which means their skeletons are made of cartilage, not bone. Cartilage is a type of connective tissue that is softer than bone. Humans have cartilage in their ears and nose.

The shortfin mako is the fastest shark in the ocean. It can swim in bursts as fast as forty-six miles per hour.

SHARK BITES

The whale shark is the largest shark in the sea and can grow to be as long as sixty feet.

Bluefin tuna are the largest tuna in the ocean. They have retractable fins on their bodies. Bluefin like to hunt by sight and have the sharpest vision of any bony fish in the sea. They can live up to forty years.

A bull shark can live in both fresh water and saltwater.

Mackerels have a bluish-green color on the upper side of their bodies and silver on the bottom. The upper part of a mackerel's body is covered with approximately twenty-five dark wavy stripes. These fish can survive up to twenty-five years in the wild.

An octopus has three hearts. Two of the hearts pump blood though each of the octopus's two gills. The third heart pumps blood through the octopus's body.

SHARK BITES

The tiger shark has amazing eyesight, which is why they can hunt so well at night.

A tsunami is a giant wave, or series of waves, usually caused by an undersea earthquake, landslide, or volcanic eruption. When a tsunami reaches land, it can cause massive destruction.

The earth's five oceans are the Pacific Ocean, Atlantic Ocean, Indian Ocean, Arctic Ocean, and Southern Ocean.

Jellyfish have been on the earth for millions and millions of years. They were here before dinosaurs.

The dorsal fin is the main fin that is located on the back of a fish or marine (relating to the sea) animal.

SHARK BITES

There are nine species of hammerhead shark, including scoophead and bonnethead.

The eyes of the hammerhead shark, which are on each side of its head, allow the hammerhead to look around an area more quickly than other sharks. It also has special sensors across its head that help it scan for food.

The blacktip reef shark is bluish-gray in color and is usually found in the coral reefs and shallow lagoons of the tropical Indian and Pacific Oceans.

FUR AND FUN FLY AT ANIMAL INN—
A SPA AND HOTEL FOR PETS!

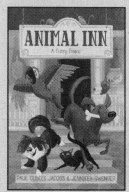

A Furry Fiasco

Treasure Hunt

The Bow-wow Bus

Bright Lights, Big Kitty!

Whooooo Done It?

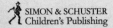